Flame of Sunset

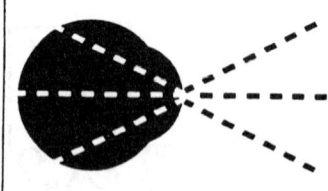

This Large Print Book carries the Seal of Approval of N.A.V.H.

Flame of Sunset

L. P. Holmes

G.K. Hall & Co.
Thorndike, Maine

Copyright © 1947 by L. P. Holmes.
Renewed ® 1975 by L. P. Holmes.
Copyright © 1948 in the British Commonwealth.

All rights reserved.

Published in Large Print by arrangement with Golden West Literary Agency.

G.K. Hall Large Print Book Series.

Printed on acid free paper in Great Britain.

Typeset in 16 pt. Plantin.

Library of Congress Cataloging-in-Publication Data

Holmes, L. P. (Llewellyn Perry), 1895–
  Flame of sunset / by L. P. Holmes.
    p. cm.
  ISBN 0-8161-5855-X (alk. paper : lg. print)
  1. Large type books. I. Title.
[PS3515.O4448F53   1994]
813'.52—dc20   93-32284
                                                   CIP

FLAME OF SUNSET

CHAPTER ONE

They came across the high Nevada desert, these gaunt and footsore cattle, the wicked sweep of their horns shining in the sun, the dust churned up by their weary hoofs lifting in a long, low drifting banner of ochre brown against the endless expanse of gray sage beyond. Their pace was slow but sure, majestically sure. For this was a herd of Destiny, earning a place in history. Nearly two thousand miles of drive trail lay behind these cattle, and the changing seasons of two full years. Their shaggy hides had known the heat of desert sun, the sleet and snow of high mountain passes, the flood waters of many a little known river. Along that wild back trail there had been the raiding fury of white and red skinned renegades, and nights when the ravening lobo wolves had prowled close and bayed an age-old hunger at the watching stars.

The great trek had begun on the Staked Plains of far off Texas. West and north these cattle streamed, cutting the Goodnight-Loving Trail above Fort Sumner, then on across New Mexico to strike the upper reaches of the Rio Grande north of old Santa Fe. Up the Rio Grande into Colorado, where the Continental Divide was crossed and the

Grand River was met and crossed and followed south along its west bank to its confluence with the Green River in Utah. Then north once more along the Green into Wyoming, then west, touching Idaho and the northwest corner of Utah before striking into Nevada and down the long, long drift beside the Humboldt, until the waters of that stream turned bitter and foul and vanished in the alkali-crusted sands and treacherous bogs of the great sink.

Beyond the Humboldt Sink lay thirst, half a hundred miles of it. But this herd had known thirst before, and the deadly, burning miles of it fell ever more and more behind until, in the dim, beckoning distance to the west lay a shimmer of green where the waters of the Truckee lived and gave life. But the men who drove the herd, at point and swing and drag, saw more than that beckoning green shimmer. They saw against the western rim of the world the lifting blue bulk of mountains, dusted with snow along the higher peaks. Here was the last land bulwark between them and their destination, the land of gold and of men's dreams.

Grizzled old Buck Yarnell, circling up from the drag, dropped in at point beside Jeff Kennett and pointed with a gaunt arm.

'That's it, Jeff,' he said, 'what we all been strainin' our eyes to see ever since we left the Panhandle. More than once along the back trail I found myself wonderin' if there was a Sierra range, if there was a Californy on the sundown side. Sittin' around the campfire I'd listen to the boys talkin' and layin' their plans and I'd get the funny feelin' that maybe it was all a pipe dream, that we'd just keep on forever and ever chasin' the sunset and never catchin' up with it. But now—well, there's the Sierras and t'other side is Californy, and I'm satisfied.'

Jeff Kennett smiled. 'I never doubted once, Buck. Either that there was such a place, or that we would reach it.'

'I know,' nodded Buck Yarnell. 'That is the youth in you. You got to get old to have doubts. And I tell you it is mighty good to a tired old man to see the home ranch finally showin' up in the distance.'

Kennett laughed softly. 'Old—and tired? Why you rawhide tough old hoot owl, you can outride and outlast any man in the crew right now, and you know it. At ninety you'll be dreaming of new country and laying plans to go take a look at it.'

A twinkle showed far back under the shaggy brows of Buck Yarnell. 'Mebbe, lad—mebbe. But I got a heap of restin' up to do, first. I've seen enough new country in the past two years to plumb dull the restless edge.'

'You'll see more before you hunker down for the rest,' promised Kennett. 'We're looking at the fringe of what we set out to reach, but we're not there yet. I'm heading out to locate a bedding ground, Buck. An awful lot of those gold crazy pilgrims have come this way. Chances are there's a heap of them camped along the Truckee right now, resting up their teams before starting the big drag over the mountains. And we don't want to turn two thousand head of long horns loose around those camps. Keep the herd driving straight along as it is now. I'll meet you again before you get there.'

Buck nodded, adding a word of caution. 'Don't you forget we're still in Shoshone country. They ain't as tough a brand of redskins as some we've met up with, but they're still tough enough not to get careless with.'

Jeff Kennett laughed again, lifted his wiry pony to a jog and began drawing steadily away from the slow plodding herd, his silver gray eyes fixed on the line of green which marked the Truckee. In time, as the miles fell behind, that distant smear of green began resolving into clumps of trees, of alder and willow, fed by the river waters. Now Kennett saw what he had reasoned he would see, signs of emigrant camps along the river banks. He picked up the pale, thin film of smoke from camp fires, glimpsed the clumsy, weathered bulk of prairie schooners, and presently movement, both human and animal.

Half a mile from the river, Kennett's pony changed from a jog to a run of its own accord, for the smell of water was in its dusty nostrils, and thirst burned deep in its vitals. Gaunt oxen, feeding ravenously in the narrow green strip of meadowland along the stream, gave grudging and ponderous way, and bearded men and gaunt women watched almost sullenly as Kennett, dismounting, held his frantic pony back from any chance of foundering itself by drinking too much and too quickly.

A lank figure of a man, his face gaunt and bitter, came striding over.

'There's the look of cattle about you, stranger,' he said bluntly. 'And we've heard word of a big herd coming in from Humboldt Sink way. Yours?'

'Mine. Why?'

'You can't bring a herd in here,' said the man. 'There ain't enough graze along here for our oxen as it is. And we got to get enough strength into our oxen to get over the hump ahead. No, you can't bring a herd in here.'

'The reasoning is correct, but the approach all wrong,' said Jeff Kennett dryly. 'Me and my men buried that word, can't, a long way back on the trail. My cattle are coming across the thirst, now. They must have water and there is plenty of that here.

But I'm looking for grass, a lot of it, and I can see that there isn't enough here. So, let's be fair both ways. The herd will come on in and drink. Then we'll head it away, either north or south, off the main emigrant trail. How does that sound to you?'

A second man had come up to listen with an ugly sullenness. He growled harshly, 'And before your herd moved on there wouldn't be a spear of grass left in these meadows. Don't let him fool you, Yount. We want no herd of cattle in here and that's final.'

Jeff Kennett, consumed with thirst himself, was crouched, scooping up water in his cupped hands, washing the bitter dust from his mouth, then drinking sparingly. He came erect, his gray eyes flashing.

'You own this water?' he rasped harshly. 'You own this country and this grass? There is only one thing final, and that is, my herd comes in and drinks. And the man who tries to stop it will wish he'd never been born. Don't get yourself out on a limb, friend—that you can't back off of.'

The sullen one dropped a hand towards the hilt of the Bowie knife in his belt, but the man Yount stopped the gesture with a sweeping arm. 'None of that, Carter! There is justice in what this rider says. The water is free—it belongs to no man alone. This thing can be arranged. Your word is good, friend—that after your herd has watered, it will be moved along?'

Jeff Kennett shrugged. 'Of course. I see thirty or forty oxen here, trying to get enough grass. There are two thousand odd head of cattle in my herd. I didn't bring that herd clear from Texas to see it starve here. I don't even intend taking my herd across the mountains by the regular traveled route, for the same reason I wouldn't try and hold it here. The wagon trains that have gone ahead are sure to have cleaned out the grass and browse along that main route. Who among you knows anything of the country to the north?'

Yount shook his head. 'None in our party. We are as new to the country as it is to you. But there is a military camp a couple of miles up river. You may get information there.'

'I'll try it,' nodded Kennett. His pony had had its fill of water by now and Kennett, looping up the reins, swung into his saddle again. 'The herd,' he went on, 'will arrive around sundown. I'll see that it is handled right.'

Riding on upstream, past the wagons and the camps, Kennett saw that here indeed were a people who had paid and were paying a heavy price for their dreams of a new land and the lure of the gold which lay there. He saw hunger, saw it in the way one woman was carefully scraping the last few pinches of flour from a limp and grimy sack, adding it to a thin and watery stew which simmered on the coals. There were children grouped about that fire, their faces pinched and old, watching that simmering pot with ravenous eyes. Yes, the price of empire was stern.

★   ★   ★

Kennett found the military camp in a side meadow, somewhat apart. It was not a big camp. A couple of officers, a dozen troopers with their saddle mounts and pack animals, comprised a party calculated to move fast and purposefully. A single small tent stood off to one side.

As Kennett was explaining himself to the trooper who stood guard, one of the officers, a lean, brisk man, came up. Kennett told him of the information he was seeking.

The officer nodded. 'I think we can be of help. We've a guide here, a mountain man who came in with us from Fort Hall. He knows this country. How big a herd are you bringing through?'

'A trifle more than two thousand head,' said Kennett.

The officer's eyes widened and he whistled softly.

Quick respect was in the glance he threw at Kennett. To the guard he said, 'Locate Benton and have him come here.'

As the guard hurried off, a peal of light,

clear laughter sounded. From over by the tent appeared a slim, feminine figure, walking with the other officer, a man of middle age, graying around the temples. Seeing the guard hurrying away, and noting Jeff Kennett talking to the junior officer, he came over, the girl with him.

'What is it, Tolbert? A report of some sort come in?'

The junior officer explained, and the older man bent a keen eyed glance at Jeff Kennett. 'That is a lot of cattle, two thousand head. What ever influenced you to start such a drive?'

Jeff shrugged. 'Down in Texas we were cattle poor. More cattle than we knew what to do with. I figured that with so many pilgrims heading for California there would probably be a shortage of eating beef. It looked like a good gamble and me and the boys decided to try it.'

'From Texas,' murmured the officer. 'All the way from Texas. An amazing achievement, Mr.—'

'Kennett—Jefferson Kennett.'

The officer put out his hand. 'I am Captain Raine. This is Lieutenant Tolbert, and—Miss Deborah Sharpe.' Captain Raine smiled down at the girl and added, 'A very wilful young lady, who, presuming on an old family friendship, influenced me to include her in this detail when we left Fort

Leavenworth.'

Miss Sharpe pouted. 'You make it sound like I was a hateful little pest, Captain. I've tried to be a good trooper.'

Raine nodded. 'And a good one you have been, Debbie. You've stood up to the hard riding and rigors of the trip like a thoroughbred. It has been very fine having you along and I'll be sorry to have to leave you at Sacramento with your father and your aunt. I'd like to take you right along with me to San Diego.'

An elfin mischief glinted in the girl's eyes. 'I'm quite sure Aunt Amanda would never agree to that, Captain. Once she gets me under her wing again, she'll keep me there. If she dreamed I was here, that I had come across the plains, she would be petrified. In her last letter to me, she said that under no conditions was I to consider coming to California.'

'Which sounds as though your aunt had not found the country very much to her liking.'

The girl smiled. 'Poor Aunt Amanda! She'll never be the same. That trip she took with Dad by boat down to Chagres and across the terrible jungle of the Isthmus, before getting another boat up to San Francisco, has done something to her. She swears that California is nothing but a land of savages, both white and red. And she ordered me not to leave Boston under any pretext.'

Captain Raine chuckled. 'I imagine I'll come in for a sound scolding for listening to the beguilements of a very disobedient young lady. However, I imagine we'll both survive.'

While they had been talking, Jeff Kennett had been studying Deborah Sharpe guardedly. He had, he thought, never seen anyone quite like her before. The women of the wagon trains he had met up with here and there along the back trail had been gaunt and tired, no doubt heroic, but with much of their feminine charm long since ground out of them by the hardships and dangers they had undergone. But this girl was fresh and pretty as a wild flower, and Jeff could see that the breath of danger was tonic to her dainty nostrils.

The girl must have felt his glance, for suddenly her eyes met his. She said gravely, 'You came up the river past those emigrant camps, Mr Kennett?'

Jeff nodded. 'Yes, ma'am. I did.'

'Then,' said Deborah Sharpe, 'perhaps you saw what I saw? Hunger in the eyes of children?'

Jeff nodded again. 'I saw it.'

'I'd like to make a bargain with you,' said the girl swiftly. 'I would like to buy several head of cattle from you, to give to those emigrant camps. They still have their oxen, but if they use them for food, they will have no way to get their wagons across the mountains. I—I will pay you a good price, Mr. Kennett.'

Jeff was not as surprised at this proposal as he might have been, for he was realizing that behind her bright charm lay all the character of keen intelligence and high, strong pride. That she would be gentle and generous as well, was to be expected. Jeff inclined his tawny head in a gesture of respect.

'I couldn't accept money from you, ma'am. But those kids will have a few square meals before they start over the mountains. I had already made up my mind to that.'

She had been watching him gravely and now her quick smile held the warmth of a direct ray of sunshine. 'That is very handsome of you, Mr. Kennett. When we start on tomorrow morning, I will have no shadow of regret riding with me. Thank you for making the last stage of my journey a pleasant one.'

Now the guard came back and with him was a lank figure in stained buckskins. When Lieutenant Tolbert explained what was wanted, the mountain guide squatted on his heels, smoothed a piece of earth with his hand and with a twig began drawing lines.

'This hyar river, the Truckee, runs north, emptyin' into a lake, a sweet water lake. You kin cross water hyar, pardner, and head yore herd of critters north along the west side of the lake. There's water and graze all the way. Above the lake there is more desert, but you don't hit that. You cut straight west at the head of the lake, and strike the mountains. The range don' run as high there as it does hyar and further south. You'll have no trouble crossin' and once you're past the main backbone you'll hit timber country that's full of meadows, grass meadows. After that it is just a case of keep going until you hit Lassen Meadows and the big valley further west. Got it?'

Kennett, studying the crude map intently, nodded. 'Indians travel that country much?'

'Some. Shoshones hang around that lake and there'll be some of the Pit tribe back in the hills. But there ain't a heap of toughness in 'em. They're a thievin' lot, but the smell of gunpowder discourages 'em quick.' The mountain man paused a moment, pulling his lip. 'Might pay to keep an eye peeled for Lobinger, though. Since the Military broke up his little game of tradin' guns to the Injuns, he's gone plumb wild. Along with a dozen—mebbe fifteen—other white renegades, he started raidin' small wagon trains along the Humboldt. But he run into a ambush and got kicked around pretty rough. I've heard some talk that since then he's been holin' up somewhere around this hyar Pyramid Lake. He's tricky, Scarface

Lobinger is. Should you meet up with him, smoke him down quick, like you would a wolf. Good luck, pardner.'

Abruptly the mountain man straightened up and prowled away, soft footed as a panther in his worn moccasins, not even waiting for the words of thanks which lay on Jeff Kennett's lips.

'Strange fellows, men like Benton,' said Lieutenant Tolbert. 'I'm not very religious but at times I think that perhaps the Lord fashioned such men deliberately, that they might ferret out the trails, the river fords, the mountain passes for the great migration to follow.'

Jeff Kennett nodded. 'There's a lot that has been done which wouldn't have been, except for men like him. Now, thank you, Lieutenant, for your help. It has been a pleasure meeting you, and you, Captain Raine, and you—Miss Sharpe. I hope the balance of your trail to Sacramento will be swift and easy.'

The officers shook hands heartily, then Jeff was a trifle startled to find Deborah Sharpe's slender hand resting in his own trail toughened palm.

'I'd still like to pay for the cattle you leave with the emigrant camps, Mr. Kennett,' she said. 'I'd like to feel that I have had some hand in smoothing their trail.'

Jeff smiled down at her. 'You have. What

was just a half formed hunch before, is now a promise. Good luck!'

'Good luck to you, Jeff Kennett!'

As Jeff swung into his saddle and rode away he carried in his mind a picture of her faintly smiling yet gravely serious face, as she spoke those final words.

* * *

The moment Jeff reached the lower meadows with their emigrant camps, he sensed the renewed animosity in the air. Off to one side a group of men were arguing heatedly and now they came over to bar his way. The man, Yount, was with them, looking distressed, rather than hostile. But there was no mistaking the mood of the knife-packing Carter, who was leading the others. He threw up an arm, warning Jeff to halt.

But Jeff did not halt, not at the moment, A thin, cold fire sharpened in his silver gray eyes and he rode right at Carter, making the fellow jump hurriedly aside. Not until Carter had given way did Jeff rein in, twisting slightly in his saddle as he looked down across the group of men.

'All right,' he rapped. 'What's twisting your tails? Same old argument, maybe?'

Yount said, 'I've tried to make them see sense, cowboy. But Carter here, he's got them in a frame of mind.'

Kennett fixed Carter with a hard stare. 'He does insist on getting further out on that limb, doesn't he?'

Carter's face suffused darkly. 'You're not out of the brush yourself, mister. We're in no mood for smart talk. Keep that herd of yours off these meadows or it will be the worse for you.'

Jeff Kennett let his glance play over the group, noted that several of the men carried rifles across their arms. He smiled faintly. 'One fool can make a dozen when they shut their minds and open their ears. The herd is coming in. I'm wondering how you figure to stop it.'

'We can stop you,' blurted Carter. 'Right here and now.'

'I can hear that limb cracking,' murmured Kennett. 'But if the rest of you have listened to Carter, maybe you'll listen to me. Be wisest, I promise you. I don't think you could stop me, right here and now, as friend Carter says. But say you did, just for the sake of argument. Then you'd have to try and stop my outfit when they came looking for me. You don't know that outfit. I do. Take Mangas Coloradas, for instance. They don't come any tougher than Mangas and his Apaches. Well, Mangas and some of his gang got considerable off their regular trail. They were prowling clear up into Northern New

Mexico when we came through. They figured to take that outfit of mine over the jumps. They tried. By the time the ruckus was over, Mangas and them that were left of his gang, were pounding the trail back for Arizona, wishing they'd stayed there in the first place. And if Mangas Coloradas and his Apaches couldn't handle my outfit, you can't. The herd is coming through!'

Before any further argument could develop, Kennett touched his pony with the spur. The men gave way before him, sullen but undecided, and before Carter could reorganize again, Jeff Kennett was past and gone.

CHAPTER TWO

Jeff Kennett met the point of the herd some four miles out from the river. He explained matters to Buck Yarnell. Buck's shadowed eyes grew frosty.

'You'd think them wagon men figured they owned the country,' he growled. 'Well, we'll knock that foolishness out of them in jig time. What's the matter with 'em, anyhow?'

'Thousands of miles of hell and hardship and danger, Buck,' answered Kennett gravely. 'And grief and hunger and all the rest of the ghosts that have been riding that trail with them. Men ain't always responsible after taking a beating like that, so we are seeing their side as well as our own. We'll swing the herd a little in the last mile before the river, and hit below the camps. We'll let the cattle take on all the water they want, cross the river and push on north along the west bank. When we bed down for the night we'll be well away from those meadows. Circle the herd and pass the word along to the boys, giving them the setup. And tell them to let me handle all argument with the wagon men.'

Buck Yarnell nodded and reined away and Jeff Kennett, heading once more toward the river, felt the resistless push of the herd as its pace picked up, now that most of the cattle could sense the nearing of water.

Toward the end, more and more of the cowboys came swinging up to the point of the herd, for no longer were drag and swing riders needed. Instead of driving the herd, their present aim was to hold it back and keep its gathering momentum from exploding into a wild stampede for the water—a stampede which could throw the weaker animals off their feet and trample them to death. The problem now was to keep that river of living flesh and blood from thundering down in a runaway tide on the river of water ahead, where floundering, frantic legs could be broken among slippery boulders, or from jumping off cut-banks, or miring down in some sluggish mudhole or backwater.

The bellowing of the herd became one long, rolling, thunderous note, deep and primitive, the volume of it dwarfing and drowning out the yipping shouts of the riders. The last quarter mile was touch and go. No human agency could possibly have stopped the herd. All Jeff Kennett and his men could do was slow the advance a little. Jeff felt as though he was riding the point of an avalanche.

The scattered mats of willows and alders along the river bank were the greatest aid. Though many of the smaller willow clumps were trampled over and smashed flat, the larger and more sturdy growth acted as a cushion against the momentum of the herd, softening it, breaking up the solid front, forcing the center of the herd to split and scatter north and south.

The first of the cattle to hit the river were forced further and further across the shallows by the surge coming in behind. But these leaders, greedy for the water, fought back, swinging up and down stream until, for hundreds of yards, the river seemed to be one of milling, gulping cattle instead of water.

Jeff Kennett and his men gathered south of the herd, thankful that the long thirst was done with, content with the knowledge that the worst of the trail was finally over. One of the riders, scooping up a hatful of water and drinking deep, sighed and wiped his dripping lips.

'Time or two I figgered that a shot of corn juice was the finest drink I ever knew,' he drawled. 'I was wrong. This is. All the way across that damned desert I been dreaming of water like this, imaginin' that I was rollin' it across my tongue, lettin' it seep wet and cool clear down into my toes. And it is, right now. I ain't a mite disappointed.'

The cattle drank long and deep, splashing up and down stream as though reluctant to leave before taking on the last gulp they could possibly hold. Then, as the bitter thirst died in them, hunger came to take its place and they left the water to hunt for grass and forage. Jeff Kennett gave crisp orders and the riders began bunching the herd again, forcing all of it across the west bank and heading it north. But some of the wilder and more stubborn animals worked fast up stream toward the emigrant camps.

Calling to a couple of his riders, Jeff spurred out to turn these strays back. They headed all but one, a perverse beast which ran like a deer. Racing after it, Jeff saw it crash into a willow clump and out the other side. And Jeff was circling the willow clump when he heard the sharp crack of a rifle, the telling thud of speeding lead striking home. He whirled into the clear just in time to see the stricken steer go down in a heap. Just across that small clearing stood several of the emigrant men, and one of them, the man Carter, was lowering a smoking rifle from his shoulder.

Jeff sped right on past the carcass of the wayward steer, straight at the emigrant men, at Carter in particular, who yelled triumphantly. 'I told you not to bring that herd—!'

Carter broke off with a curse, suddenly aware that Jeff Kennett had slid one of his belt guns free and was spurring in on him with cold anger and purpose blazing in his eyes. In panic, Carter tried to reload his rifle, but saw he would never be in time. He turned, started to run, yelling at his companions to shoot, to use their loaded weapons on this avenging horseman coming in so fast.

But now other riders had sped into view behind Jeff Kennett and in face of this support, the emigrant men hesitated. Carter, seeing there was no help from them and knowing he could not hope to outrun Jeff's horse, turned and snatched out his Bowie knife.

He had no chance to use it, for Jeff was already close upon him. Jeff swung his gun before Carter could swing the knife. The heavy barrel of the weapon clipped Carter across the side of his bullet head, knocking him spinning to the ground in a senseless heap. Then Jeff had set his pony up into a rearing, whirling stop, the muzzle of his gun taking in the sullen group with restless, stabbing authority.

'You fools!' Jeff cried. 'You stupid, pig-headed fools! How you ever found brains enough to get this far is beyond me. Don't any of you get ideas with those guns! I'm about through fooling with you. Where's Yount?'

'Back at the camp,' muttered one of the group sullenly. 'But—'

'Go get him!' ordered Jeff. 'He's the only one of you fit to be running loose. Go get him!'

The fellow turned and slouched away. One of the others said, 'Don't blame John Yount for this. This was Carter's idea and—maybe the rest of us weren't thinking any too fast. Is Carter—?'

'No,' rapped Jeff. 'He's not dead. It would have taken a harder wallop than I gave him to crack his thick head. But maybe I've knocked some sense into him.'

At this moment Buck Yarnell came spurring up, drawn by the sound of the shot. He took a look at the dead steer, then at Jeff, holding the group of emigrant men under his ready gun. Buck jerked a grizzled head at the figure of Carter and growled, 'Why stop at just one, Jeff? Work 'em over!'

'The one that had it coming most, got it,' said Jeff. 'I think the trouble is done with. Take a couple of the boys and start picking up about a dozen of the most sore footed critters you can find. Bunch them and bring them up river towards the wagon camps.'

Yarnell stared, then a queer, understanding light gleamed in his eyes. 'You,' he said gruffly, 'will never get over being soft headed. But I love you for it.'

Buck rode off, just as John Yount and the man who had gone after him, appeared. Yount took a long look around, then shrugged, his glance meeting that of Jeff's. 'I tried to tell them,' he said simply.

'I know,' said Jeff. 'I'm going to make you a present, Yount. When I first rode through your camps I saw something in the eyes of women and kids that no decent man likes to see. I saw hunger. That steer yonder that Carter shot, is yours. Take it, dress it out, and see that those women and kids eat, and eat plenty. I'm having a dozen more critters rounded up which I'm giving to you personally, Yount, for I can see you're a good man. Those critters will keep the women and kids from being hungry crossing the hump ahead. You can't afford to slaughter any of your oxen, for you need them to haul your wagons. But from here on in, you'll at least have meat.'

All of the listening group grew very still, so still that the mumbled curse which broke from Carter's lips as he got to wavering feet, blinking a return to his senses, sounded like a harsh snarl. He swung around, feet spread, head rolling from side to side.

'My knife,' he mumbled. 'Where's my knife? I'll cut his heart out. I'll—'

'You'll shut your stupid gab and keep it shut, Jase Carter,' growled one of the group. 'Listening to you has made us about as big a bunch of fools as ever came cross the plains. You make another move toward knife work and I'll shoot you down with my own hand. If your wife and kids don't starve to death going across the mountains, it will be because of the generosity of the very man you'd have used a knife on. Yes, you shut your gab!'

The anger had left Jeff Kennett's eyes. Now he smiled slightly and put away his gun.

'I reckon there's no quarrel left between us. I wish you luck all the rest of the way down the trail.'

He would have reined away, but John Yount stepped up, one gaunt arm extended.

'Shake,' he said. 'The meat will be used as you would wish it to be. My word on that. You'll be mentioned in the prayers of women and kids this night. I had hoped to maybe be able to buy one critter from you, for I too have watched that hunger, watched it over many a weary mile. If payment of any sort—'

Jeff Kennett shook his tawny head, thinking of the words of a girl who had also seen that hunger and had wanted generously to do something about it. He remembered the warmth and directness of her smile.

'I've already been paid,' he said, wringing Yount's hand.

★　　★　　★

On the west border of the sweet water lake of which the mountain man had told him, Jeff Kennett and his men held the herd for a week. Guards were always on duty and, more than once, in the distance, they glimpsed wary, slinking figures.

'Shoshones,' growled Buck Yarnell. 'They need keeping an eye on, but they haven't got much taste for real rough work. No sign yet of that Scarface Lobinger hombre you were tellin' us about, Jeff.'

'That mountain man, Benton, did not say we would run into Lobinger,' said Jeff. 'He only said we might. Yet, you seldom see a snake until it is right up close to you, so we won't make the mistake of getting careless.'

With the herd full fed, rested and some of the gauntness gone from it, the drive was renewed in the pale gray dawn of a clear morning and the riders whooped exuberantly as they bunched the herd and started it moving once more to the beckoning, luring west. They crossed sageland, even thirst again, but thirst of short duration, for now the first foothills of the Sierras were at hand, and little streams came down out of the timbered steeps, mountain water, clear and cold and sweet, where myriads of trout darted and fed in singing shallows, or lay still with slow winnowing fins in the depths of some deep shaded pool.

Out ahead of the herd Jeff Kennett rode, sometimes alone, generally with the grizzled wisdom of Buck Yarnell at his shoulder, working out the easiest trail for the following cattle. Finally, the day came when they found the pass Benton had told Jeff they would find and that night they bedded the herd just below the east mouth of it. Around the campfire Jeff told his riders of the pass.

'This time tomorrow night, boys, we'll be lookin' down the other side—we'll be heading down hill for a change. Water that starts down any creek on the other side ends up in that Pacific Ocean we been hearing about. What we set out to see, we're going to see.'

A gaunt rider said, 'I aim to take a good look, not only for myself, but for Johnny Beckwith and Mose Carr and Jeddy Tobit and Tim Burke. It wasn't in the cards, I reckon, for them boys to have made it through with the rest of us, but they were shore aimin' to have a good look at this Californy and I figger the next best thing to them seein' it for themselves, is for me to see it for 'em.'

The group went silent, staring at the flames. The men named had been buried along the trail.

Old Buck Yarnell found the answer they were searching for.

'We never let those boys down. We put through a drive that plenty of men said couldn't be done, a drive they can date time from. As far as they got, Johnny and Mose and Jeddy and Tim were part of it, and they wouldn't have had us turn back when their strings ran out. We didn't. We came on through. I think—I'm sure, those boys would have liked that. How about it, Jeff?'

Jeff Kennett nodded gravely. 'Yes. They would have liked that.'

★ ★ ★

In the frosty dawn, Jeff and Buck were out ahead of the herd again. A few hundred yards below the east mouth of the pass, Jeff reined in abruptly and pointed down at the soft forest mat under the age old timber. Buck Yarnell looked, grunted and swung swiftly from his saddle, prowled back and forth, bent over as he studied the fresh turned sign.

'Horses,' he growled. 'Nigh on to a dozen of them. That sign wasn't here when we was up here yesterday, Jeff. What do you make of it?'

Jeff was swinging a wary head. 'Hard telling, yet. Maybe Indians, maybe Scarface Lobinger, maybe mountain men. Mostly I'm thinking that there is a pass ahead, a high pass where the timber runs out and lets rock and scrub-brush take over. A beautiful trap, if we were in the middle, for guns laying in wait on each side. We don't start through that pass until we've looked things over. Buck, hit back to the herd. Leave just two men at drag. Tell them not to push the herd a bit, but just hold it from heading back down grade again. Bring the rest of the boys back with you. I'll wait right here for you.'

By the time Buck Yarnell returned with the men, Jeff had figured out his tactics. He split the group into two and said, 'Buck, you and I have a look at the pass. You take the south, I'll take the north. Circle back a mile or so, then hit for the top. When you get there, come up on the south flank. I'll be doing the same on the north. If any gang is holed up to jump us in the pass, we'll have them between us. Should they be there, make the lesson good. We don't want to be fighting our way clear across these mountains. We might as well settle the issue right here and now.'

Buck nodded grimly. 'Let's ride.'

An hour later Jeff led his little group into a jack-pine filled hollow on the side of the gaunt rock peak which looked down on the north flank of the pass. They dismounted and, leaving one man to guard the horses, Jeff and the other four went out on foot, ducking through thickets, skirting ledge and steep.

Presently, they were able to look down and across the pass. And there, at the head of a shallow gulch, Jeff glimpsed movement. Six horses, saddle mounts, were tethered in the gulch. But no men were anywhere to be seen.

Stony Peters, at Jeff's elbow, muttered, 'What we're lookin' for will be over the ridge on the far side of the gulch, closer to the pass. After all, they're figgerin' to surprise and trap us, not have us trap and surprise them.'

'We'll go in,' Jeff said.

They dropped warily into the gulch, guns ready for instant work, and went up the other side, some seventy-five yards below the horses. Nearing the crest they flattened out, creeping like Indians, silent and grimly purposeful.

Pulling himself up and across a ledge of weather darkened granite, Jeff suddenly found himself looking at the head and shoulders of a man not ten feet distant! Prescience, instinct, perhaps some faintest of sounds made the fellow turn his head and stare straight into Jeff Kennett's eyes. Then, before Jeff could move, the fellow fell, rather than leaped, down the far side of the ledge and his wild bawl of warning echoed thinly across the pass.

Jeff lunged ahead until he could look over and down. He saw the sadly startled renegade, who had no doubt been posted as a lookout higher up to warn those below of the expected advance of the herd, racing down the slope in wild, clumsy leaps. And each leap brought forth another warning yell. Then further down, where the slope swelled out in a tangle of rock and scrub growth before breaking off into the pass proper, Jeff glimpsed men scurrying and scrambling, seeking cover from attack from the rear, where they had obviously expected to need cover only to hide them from the pass.

'Here they are, like we expected,' Jeff called over his shoulder. 'White renegades. Spread out and take your time. We got 'em where we want 'em!'

Pushing his rifle ahead of him, Jeff edged out again until he could look down into the gut of the pass. A rifle spanged, and then another, and Jeff felt the wind of one bullet past his face. But he saw the fellow who had fired that second shot, saw him only partially hidden in a tangle of brush and rocks. And when Jeff's rifle steadied and spat, the renegade lurched fully erect, spun around and dropped out of sight.

Over on Jeff's right sounded the voice of Stony Peters.

'Real old Texas rifle work, that was, Jeff. You beat me to that hombre by a finger-wiggle. I was just thinning my sights on him when you shot. They don't hide near as good as Mangas Coloradas and his Apaches did. Oh—oh! There's anoth—' The rest of Stony's words were blotted out by the crash of his rifle. Down below a renegade gave a thin, high cry of agony, and Jeff knew that Stony had scored.

Jeff was morally certain that these renegades were the Scarface Lobinger gang, and as such, deserved no slightest hint of mercy. Back there to the misty east, way out in the Nevada desert, where the turgid waters of the Humboldt ran, such men had struck more than one wagon train for murder and loot.

His rifle reloaded, Jeff looked for another target. He saw it, just as one of his men, higher up the ridge, loosed a shot. Jeff saw the renegade jerk under the impact of the unerring lead, then melt down into a still heap. This was too much for the renegades on the north side of the pass. They broke and raced down into the pass proper, heading for the south side. And way over there rifles began to crack and scattered bullets began striking along the slope of the ridge in spiteful thuds, covering the flight of the nearer renegades.

Only chance could bring about a hit at this range. Jeff got to his feet and started down the slope. 'Come on,' he yelled. 'Let's go after them. Buck and the other boys are due to buy into this any time now, and that will be surprise number two for that gang. Come on. Keep after them!'

They went down the steep slope in long, sliding leaps, broke through the tangle of rocks and brush where the renegades had tried to hole up, and hit the smoothly curving slope which led to the floor of the pass.

It was then that Buck Yarnell and his stout lads bought into the fight. From the heights above the south side of the pass they announced their arrival by a mingled volley of lead and shrill Texas yells which brought fear stricken confusion to the renegades. Running figures broke down into the pass and raced toward the west and on these clear targets Jeff and Stony and the others went to work, though the range was still long for that kind of shooting.

Jeff heard Stony growl a curse as he fired and missed, but one of the other cowboys brought down a fleeing renegade in a long, rolling sprawl. Jeff selected a target of his own, swung the sights smoothly ahead and fired. He saw the fellow jackknife in mid-air as though he had struck some invisible barrier. Then, from the corner of his eye, Jeff saw a figure rear up from a copse of dwarf, storm-beaten aspen, not ten yards away. Jeff whirled to find the round, blue eye of a gun settling into line with his heart. Behind the gun was a broad, malignant face, branded indelibly by a great, livid scar, curving from above one ear down and into the scraggy beard which only partly hid the snarling mouth.

These two things Jeff Kennett saw, in one split second glance, the eye of the gun, and the scar on the face behind it. He dropped, dropped faster than he ever had before in his life, and the bullet which, in a licking gust of pale flame, leaped from the muzzle of the gun, ripped open the tip of his hat crown as cleanly as would the stroke of a knife. Jeff's own rifle was empty and he had dropped it even before he struck the rocky earth. But his belt guns were out and stabbing level, as he lurched back to his knees. Jeff smashed out two shots, but the second shot was not needed. Scarface Lobinger was dead, sprawled in the twisted, dwarf aspens.

CHAPTER THREE

Six weeks later Jeff rode through a low, wet tule fog which spread in a gray blanket over all the lowlands of the great central valley of California. Off to the west, somewhere, ran the great, amber, smoothly sliding river. Jeff had been roughly paralleling the Sacramento for the past two days, on the advice of a gaunt, buckskin clad mountaineer he had met shortly after coming out of the Sierra foothills below Lassen Meadows. By keeping the river always at his right hand, so the mountaineer had said, Jeff could not miss coming in time to the roaring town which was the heart of the gold country, the town which bore the same name as the river. The river, Jeff knew, was not too distant, for several times the hoarse wail of a steamboat whistle sounded through the fog.

After the fight at the pass with Scarface Lobinger's renegade band, the balance of the drive into Lassen Meadows had gone without noteworthy incident. Finally they had struck the great spread of Lassen Meadows with their plentiful water and grass, while from a point not much further west they looked out over a great, misted gulf which told them that here at last was the heart valley of California. They had been content to stop there and consider their course of action.

It was finally agreed that the soundest plan would be for Jeff to go on ahead and locate ways and means of getting the cattle to a market in the fabulous city of San Francisco, where, so they had heard, men were mad with the fever of gold and would be willing to pay out that gold most generously for fresh beef, Texas beef. So now Jeff was far down in the heart of the great valley boring through the fog and wishing that he might have met with clearer weather for this initial ride across the raw, new California country. But the fog continued to guard its secrets jealously and all Jeff could tell was that for mile after mile his horse's hoofs cut into lush flats and meadows where the wild grasses grew so tall as to brush across his stirrups. From time to time great spreading oak trees loomed through the fog, dim and spectral and dripping.

It was while he reined up momentarily beside one of these to breath his pony that Jeff heard, off to his left, the skirl and rattle of wheels, the jangle of trace and the muffled roll of hoofs. Jeff reined that way and presently his mount, snorting relief at finding something which offered definite direction, moved out along a narrow road. Of its own accord the wiry cow-pony struck up a jog, following the sound of that wheeled conveyance ahead.

Jeff Kennett knew a certain relief, himself. It was good to feel that he was at last getting somewhere close to human habitation, and he was content merely to keep within hearing distance of that wheeled conveyance ahead. But abruptly came the squeal of brakes and the sound of rolling wheels ceased. Voices sounded, muffled by the fog, harsh voices, with a note of violence in them. Jeff swung his pony off the road into the lush, fog wet grass which muffled the sound of its advancing hoofs. He leaned forward a trifle in his saddle, eyes and ears straining to pierce the gray, mocking blanket which shrouded everything so densely.

Again came that sound of voices, and the note of violence was a steadily mounting threat. A bitter, explosive curse was followed by the pale wink of gun-flame, the thud of a shot, and a heavy, muffled, thumping fall. And now, through the coiling fog, Jeff made out the high wheeled, unmistakable outline of a thoroughbrace stage. He sent his pony edging steadily closer, drawing a belt gun as he advanced. He saw the figures of two men, one on either side of the stage.

He heard a heavy growl of command, a frightened cry, then a clear, indignant, feminine voice. He saw one of the men reach into the stage. There was a short struggle before the possessor of that feminine voice was dragged out into the roadway, fighting furiously. The ruffian who held her, laughed hoarsely, mocking her struggles, but the laugh broke off into a snarl of fury as she managed to break away from him. She ran straight back toward where Jeff Kennett sat his restless bronc. Cursing his anger, the renegade leaped after her and Jeff heard her despairing little wail as the fellow quickly overhauled her. Jeff sent his pony lunging forward and his voice reached out, crisp and sure.

'This way—ma'am—this way!'

He vaguely glimpsed the white oval of her face as he sped past her. The renegade, startled at sight of this ghostly horseman bearing down on him out of the fog, stopped short and threw up a gun. But Jeff, alert and watching for just such a move, shot first, driving a bullet home into the very center of the renegade's chest. The fellow coughed thickly, spun around and collapsed.

Jeff swung his pony sharply, sent it lunging across the road, close behind the stage, where he nearly rode down the second renegade, who was circling back at a run. The fellow tried to dodge, but Jeff's stirruped boot pushed shrewdly out, caught the man in the stomach, spinning him around, slamming him hard against the side of the stage, causing him to drop the gun he held. As Jeff set up his pony in a rearing turn, the renegade, all fight knocked out of him, plunged heavily off into the fog. Jeff let him go.

Swinging back around the stage, Jeff met that slim, feminine figure coming slowly along the road. She was sobbing a little and Jeff, alarmed, dismounted and stood beside her.

'You're not hurt, ma'am?' he asked.

But her pain was of anger, more than anything else. 'My feelings are,' she flared. 'Those filthy, murderous brutes! Look how that—that animal tore my dress. It's my best one. Aunt Amanda bought it for me just yesterday. There isn't another like it in all California. And that beast, with his filthy claws, tore it—' Her words broke off abruptly, as she stared at Jeff with widening eyes. 'Why—why,' she stammered. 'It's you—Jefferson Kennett—!'

The last time Jeff had seen this girl was far back across the mountains, at the military camp on the Truckee River. 'Well, well, Miss Sharpe,' Jeff drawled. 'We get around, don't we—you and I? But I wouldn't worry too much about that dress. All I can see is just a little tear in one sleeve.'

Deborah Sharpe, recovering her initial surprise of recognition, retorted with some emphasis. 'You don't understand. The dress will never be the same. And after all of Aunt Amanda's trouble and kindness—Oh! I'd forgotten all about poor Aunt Amanda—!'

Away she flew, on twinkling feet, back to the stage into which she climbed with vigorous activity. Jeff moved after her and looked in at the open door. An older, stoutish woman was in there, slumped in a corner and Deborah Sharpe was rubbing and patting the older woman's limp hands.

'Fainted, that's all,' the girl explained. 'She'll be all right shortly. Such affairs as this simply don't happen in Boston. When she comes to, she'll be almost disappointed to find she hasn't been scalped, for she's been more than half expecting such a fate ever since she arrived in this wild, ruffian filled wilderness. So she claims, at least.'

The girl seemed to have totally recovered from her experience. Something almost like mischief twinkled in her brown eyes as she explained about her Aunt Amanda.

'She can have a couple of dead men if she wants them,' said Jeff Kennett dryly. 'That one that was after you. And here's another by the off front wheel who must have been the stage driver.'

He saw swift contriteness sweep over her. 'I—I'm a little beast, worrying about a torn dress, when—when ... That poor driver—I heard the shot, heard him fall ... Is there something we can do for him?'

Jeff shook his head. 'No more than to see that he is buried by friends. This stage—where is it headed?'

'For Sacramento. We've come from Marysville.'

'How far to Sacramento?'

'I—I can't be rightly sure. Riding through this fog for hours and hours, one loses all sense of time and distance. But it can't be much farther. Only—how will we get there, with that poor driver—?'

'I'll drive the stage in,' said Jeff. 'Can't leave you stranded here. You take care of your aunt and we'll be on our way.'

* * *

In his time, Jeff Kennett had seen a number of boom towns, but never anything to match the boiling, surging tide of raw vitality, the seething admixture of human types and races, that was Sacramento. The streets were aswirl with life. Miners, prospectors, gold hunters of all types jostled sailing men from all countries of the world, who had jumped ship in San Francisco harbor and headed for the Sierra foothills, drawn by the lure of gold. Haughty, elegant Spanish dons matched strides with shuffling Chinese coolies. Gentlemen and scoundrels, honest men and thieves, gamblers, touts, boomers, promoters, speculators—all were part of Sacramento. Freight wagons heaved ponderously through the chuck holes of the streets. Prairie schooners were there, creaking and weather blasted. And over all was a steady, rumbling vitality of sound, the voice of the sprawling, tumultuous river town.

Early dusk was falling by the time Jeff Kennett brought the stage rolling safely in. A stockily built man with a mop of shaggy red hair came hustling out of the stage station. The rumble of his voice reached up angrily at Jeff, through the thickening dusk.

'You're late, Simes. You're over an hour late. I told you before—' The red-headed man broke off in astonishment as Jeff swung down from the box to confront him. Then he blurted, 'And who in hell are you? Where's Joe Simes, my driver? What—?'

'One at a time, friend—and I'll find the answers,' broke in Jeff bluntly. 'Me—I'm Jeff Kennett. Your driver, I reckon, is the dead man I got tied on the luggage boot. He tangled with a couple of holdups, back along the trail a piece, and got shot. Too bad.'

The dumbfounded redhead followed Jeff around to the rear of the stage, took a look at the gruesome freight and mumbled, 'That's Joe Simes, all right. You say there was a holdup? Where—?'

Swift suspicion leaped into the man's eyes and Jeff seeing it, said crisply, 'Don't be a fool! I had no part in it, except to bust it up. I got one of the holdups, evening up for your driver. I went to the trouble of bringing the stage in because there's a couple of lady passengers in it. I couldn't leave them stranded out in that everlasting fog.'

At this moment a gleaming carriage, driven by a liveried servant, came spinning up. Out of it stepped a spare, tall man, who carried himself with military, ramrod straightness. He was dressed in quiet elegance, his careful grooming extending to the very tip of his impeccably trimmed gray goatee, above which flashed a pair of cold blue eyes. There was a crackle in his voice as he said to the redhead, 'I'm expecting my daughter and my sister on this stage, Hankins. Where are they?'

'Right here, Dad,' called the clear young voice of Deborah Sharpe. Opening the stage door, she stood poised. 'You'll have to give me a hand with Aunt Amanda, I'm afraid. She is still upset over the holdup.'

'Holdup! What holdup?'

'Looks like somebody tried it, Colonel Sharpe,' said the redhead. 'They killed my driver, Joe Simes. This feller here, Jeff Kennett he calls himself, brought the stage in.'

Now Colonel Sharpe saw the body of the driver and his cold eyes flashed angrily. 'You should guard your stages more carefully, Hankins. Deborah and her aunt might have been hurt.'

'They might have been,' drawled Jeff Kennett, 'but they weren't. This poor devil,' and he jerked a nod at the body of the stage driver, 'got hurt—plenty. But maybe, being just a stage driver, he don't count.'

Colonel Sharpe's flashing glance fixed on Jeff, who met the look coolly. 'It was part of his job to take risks,' rapped the colonel.

'Maybe,' shrugged Jeff. 'But I reckon he could have avoided this danger had he chose to knuckle under—easy. But he tried to put up a fight to protect his passengers, so the holdups shot him. He must have been a pretty good man, Joe Simes.'

A tinge of color showed in the colonel's face. 'Yes—yes, of course,' he snapped. He turned to the redhead. 'Was any Marysville gold coming out on this stage, Hankins?'

Hankins shook his head. 'None at all, Colonel. The gold stages generally carry a guard.'

'The outlaw element would know that, of course. And with this stage carrying no gold, they would have had no cause to bother it. Unless this affair was engineered by Ballinger, to hit at me through my daughter and my sister.' The colonel's eyes narrowed as he thought over this possibility. Then, with a shrug, he turned and stepped up to where the girl stood waiting in the door of the stage. Hankins, the redhead, growled under his breath.

'He's crazy, making that kind of talk. Bill Ballinger don't fight that way, by pickin' on women. This holdup was just one of those things.' Jeff Kennett was untying the lead rope of his saddle pony, and now Hankins turned to him, saying, 'Sorry if I jumped to fool conclusions, Kennett. I owe you plenty for bringing in this stage for me, and I'm thanking you. Any time I can return the favor, just count on me. Shake!'

Jeff gripped the extended hand and nodded. 'Forget it. Glad I happened along. One thing you can do. Tell me where I might find this feller—Bill Ballinger.'

Hankins scratched his red thatch. 'That,' he said, 'is quite an order. You might find Captain Bill Ballinger anywhere from Red Bluff to San Francisco. One thing is dead sure—he won't be far from boats and water. Another thing, almost as sure, you won't find him far from trouble. Bill has a yen for both. Just the same, you'll find him as square a man as ever bucked the tide. Sorry I can't point you definite. Your best bet at finding him would be to go down along the river front and ask the first man you see if Captain Bill Ballinger is around. If he is, just about everybody will know it.'

By this time Colonel Nathaniel Sharpe had lifted his daughter down from the stage. Now the two of them were aiding the descent of Aunt Amanda. The elder lady, fat and fussy, was declaiming, at considerable length and with decided shrillness, her opinion of this ghastly wilderness of California and the unspeakable ruffians who peopled it. She was helped across and into the waiting carriage, still venting her opinions.

The colonel was about to give his daughter a hand up into the carriage when the girl said something to him, turned and came swiftly over to Jeff Kennett, who was just reaching for a stirrup, ready to mount. She stood before Jeff, poised and breathless, and her face, as she looked up at him, was a soft, warm cameo in the murky dusk.

'I want to thank you, Jeff Kennett,' she told him gravely, 'for your gallantry and kindness. I—I am not as heartless as I might have seemed. I feel very badly about that poor driver. It was not very kind of me to be worrying about a silly dress while he lay—lay dead. I'm not that way—really.' Her hand lay briefly in his and her lips parted in a small and dawning smile. 'I think you are the nicest man I ever met, Jeff Kennett,' she said, then ran for the carriage, light and swift as a bird.

Jeff stood, hat in hand, watching the carriage disappear into the fog-laden dusk. He turned to the redhead.

'Another little favor, Hankins. How's to leave my bronc in your corral?'

'Done!' said Hankins. 'And you can leave your gear in my office. It will be safe there.'

★   ★   ★

The dark was coming down fast by the time Jeff reached the river front and here life ran in an even more surging restless tide than it did further up town. Lights were now beginning to burn through the murk of fog and darkness, and riverfront saloons and gambling dives were doing a rushing business. A dark coated gambler showed in front of Jeff, who accosted him gravely.

'Maybe you could tell me where I might find Captain Bill Ballinger, friend?'

The gambler nodded. 'I hear he is bringing the new boat, *Mother Lode*, up from San Francisco, and I think that was a new whistle which sounded just a few minutes ago. You get to know the tone of them. And this one is new. It is probably the *Mother Lode* and should be coming in now to tie up any moment. Tricky business in this fog, but if any man can do it right, Bill Ballinger can. When you meet him, tell him that Harry Travers wishes him luck.'

Jeff thanked the gambler and went on, mingling with the crowd gathered along the river bank. Sure enough, down the river a bit, almost indistinguishable through the fog, were floating lights and the slow, measured splashing of a paddle wheel. Then a whistle blared, deep and sonorous. Bells clanked and a great, resonant voice shouted orders.

'That's Bill,' said a man in the crowd. 'He knows how to keep those deckhands jumping. Ten dollars says he lays her dead on the first try.'

Someone took up the bet and partisans for either side argued and jeered.

The whistle sent its roar splintering through the fog again and now Jeff could make out the superstructure of the steamboat sliding up through the murk. Alternately the paddle wheel thumped and foamed and then was still, in answer to those jangling bells.

Steadily the advancing boat loomed clearer. Then suddenly there was a yell of warning and a burst of excitement further up the river front. A second boat was gliding down stream, apparently heading for the same berth as the *Mother Lode*.

'It's Carlin!' bawled a man in the crowd. 'It's Captain Noah Carlin. He's aimin' to mess up the *Mother Lode*'s first landing, and that'll put a curse on the new boat.'

'Bill will ride him under,' yelled another. 'Bill will ride him under—sure!'

Now the two boats were in sight of each other. From the *Mother Lode* came a series of short, rumbling whistle blasts. But the down river boat came steadily on. A collision seemed inevitable.

Out of the wheel house of the *Mother Lode* came a roar of wrath with carrying power second only to the whistle above.

'Get that rotten tub out of the way or I'll grind you under, Carlin! I'm coming in to berth and all the whelps in Nate Sharpe's kennels can't stop me. Give me leeway or I'll grind you under!'

There was no change in the course of the down river boat, so now deep in the *Mother Lode* those jangling bells sounded again with a definite, crackling authority. The paddle wheel began to thud and pound, faster and faster and the towering bulk of the *Mother Lode* seemed to lunge forward in a mad charge.

Jeff Kennett found himself holding his breath. It seemed inevitable to him that the two boats must crash, head on. Then at the last second the down river boat swung away, out into the clear channel of the river and slid by, with only a scant yard or so separating the two cargo decks.

From the wheel house of the *Mother Lode* that great voice roared taunts and jibes. Bells jangled again and the paddle wheel of the *Mother Lode* reversed and beat river waters to foam with pounding, gargantuan smacks. The *Mother Lode* shivered and slowed, sidled in to the bank, exhaust hissing and blowing. Throwing lines snaked out from the cargo deck, fore and aft. Eager hands on the bank caught them and dragged in dripping mooring hawsers, looping them about handy tree stumps. Then, ponderously, but with a strange, nestling confidence, the *Mother Lode* sidled up to the bank and was secured. A final roaring, triumphant burst from the whistle signaled a true and masterful landing.

Spontaneous cheers broke from the crowd and the man who had made the ten dollar bet, collected it gleefully.

'I told you Bill would do it. Best captain on the river. Any time Noah Carlin thinks he can bluff Bill Ballinger, he better think twice.'

A gangplank was run out from the boat to the bank and a hurrying crowd of passengers came streaming off. Most of them were gold seekers who paused neither to look around nor ask questions, but just hurried away into the fog, drawn by the everlasting lure of fabled gulch and wash.

Now that the excitement was over, the crowd began breaking up and drifting away, for the night air was dank and chill. Soon Jeff Kennett was virtually alone, except for an occasional river loafer, shuffling by. Jeff went over to the gangplank and was about to cross to the boat when a huge figure of a man came striding off the *Mother Lode*, a man who was humming cheerfully to himself as his bare head and open throated blue wool shirt challenged the wet chill of the fog-laden dark.

'I'm looking for Captain Bill Ballinger,' Jeff said.

The big man slowed his stride. 'You've found him. What can I do for you, stranger?'

'I've a business deal to talk over,' said Jeff. 'But you'd probably be mainly interested in knowing that it was Long Dave Mowrie who suggested I look you up.'

'Long Dave Mowrie!' ejaculated Ballinger. 'That restless old mountain cat. Where'd you bump into Dave?'

'Up below Lassen Meadows. He said he was on his way to take a look at the Oregon country.'

'He would be! Dave Mowrie can't stay in one place long enough to wash his ears. If you're a friend of his, you're a friend of mine. I didn't get the name.'

'Kennett—Jeff Kennett.'

'Shake, Kennett. Glad to know you.'

It was like shaking hands with a bear. Jeff stood an even six foot in his socks, but he had to look up to meet the eyes of Captain Bill Ballinger, who said, 'I got some cargo ladings and other reports to deliver. Come along. I get this business cleaned up, we'll come back on the boat where we can talk in peace. Had supper yet?'

'Not yet,' Jeff admitted.

'Fine! You'll eat with me and we'll do our talking then.'

CHAPTER FOUR

The steamboat office was not far away and Jeff waited outside until Ballinger finished making his report. Then the two of them started back for the river front.

'Those spineless pups in the office!' Ballinger growled. 'Tried to give me a calling down for risking a collision with Noah Carlin and that rotten old hulk he skippers, the *Gold Camp*. What would they have had me do, let him scare me out of a berthing? Fine finish that would have been for the *Mother Lode*'s maiden trip. Bah! They disgust me, that lilylivered breed. How do they expect to hold their own against Colonel Nate Sharpe's crowd, unless they stand up and fight?'

Captain Bill's voice ran off into a series of rumbles and growls not unlike the mutterings of a volcano about to erupt. Jeff Kennett did not answer, but he smiled grimly into the darkness. He liked this big man, this Captain Bill Ballinger. Here was a two-fisted battler who would never back up an inch.

Ballinger, still simmering with wrath, did not mark the sudden slither and shift of massed movement in the fog-choked darkness. But Jeff Kennett did and a little prickle of warning ran up his spine. He swung his head, straining eyes and ears.

'Look out, Captain Bill!'

He had hardly time to rap out the quick warning when the darkness spawned a charging group of men, who came racing in on them with a swift pound of running feet. The next moment Jeff Kennett found himself in the midst of a swirling, battling group, aiming their blows and curses mainly at Captain Ballinger, but swiftly including Jeff himself in the vicious attack.

A heavy fist crashed to the side of Jeff's skull, dropping him to his knees, filling his head with numbing shock and his eyes with a vast display of shooting stars and weird lights. For a little time he stayed there on his knees, shaking his dazed head, fighting off the momentary paralyzing shock which seemed to weigh down his muscles with lead. Then he lunged erect, driven by a cold fury. He glimpsed a snarling, cursing face and hit it, driving in his fist with the rolling power of his shoulders. He felt flesh pulp and give under his hard-ridged knuckles and the face fell away from him. He saw two more faces, pale and menacing in the fog and gloom, and he hit them with the same tigerish power.

Jeff now found himself standing free and alone. Down on the black earth about him he heard men retching and groaning. But out there ahead was still a battling group, a swirling, wild tangle of combat and in the center of it the great voice of Captain Bill Ballinger still roared its wrath and defiance.

Lean and deadly, Jeff Kennett charged in. He picked targets and hit them. He took blows in return and shook them off, armored now with that bitter fury which seemed to make him impervious to pain and shock. His own blood ran down his face across his mouth and chin, but he spat its warm saltiness from his battered lips and bored in with ferocious purpose. He fought his way right to the side of Captain Bill and added a shrill and taunting Texas yell to Ballinger's challenging bellow.

The attacking ardor of the gang began to wane. Definitely they were getting more than they bargained for. Against either of these men alone they might have won by sheer weight of numbers. But with the two of them now fighting back to back they were making doubtful progress.

A hard and bitter voice urged the gang to greater effort and a burly, rawboned figure came charging in from the side. Jeff, glimpsing this attack, pivoted slightly and drove a whistling blow which started from his very toes. The shock of landing that blow left Jeff's fist and wrist and arm partially numb, but the raw-boned figure sagged back and disappeared under the punishing impact. But now a deadlier element showed. Jeff caught the faint gleam of naked steel.

Captain Bill saw it, too. 'That knife, look out for that knife, Kennett!' he yelled.

Jeff was looking out. He was also drawing one of those big Walker Model Colt guns which sagged at his hips. He lashed out with it, crashing the heavy barrel of the weapon down on the head of the wouldbe knife wielder. The fellow went down silently, limply, his skull crushed.

That ended it. The gang broke and ran, leaving Jeff and Captain Bill standing there victorious. A savage rage still burned in Jeff and he would have charged after the fleeing roughs, but Bill Ballinger's big hand dropped on his shoulder and held him.

'Easy, friend—easy! There's more than one knife in that crowd and in the dark a knife can be bad business. We're getting out of here before they come back with twice as many. This way!'

They were soon at the river bank, with the bulk of the *Mother Lode* towering above them. As they crossed the gangplank, Captain Bill called to a deck hand.

'Get yourself a pick handle, Mike, and let no one across who hasn't business here. If they argue, knock 'em on the head and throw 'em overboard. If Colonel Nate Sharpe and Captain Noah Carlin and company want to play the game this rough—why, by gravy, they get it rough!'

They climbed the ladder to the captain's cabin, turned up the lamp and surveyed each other. Captain Bill's broad, square jawed, leathery face broke into a swollen grin as he tenderly fingered an eye that was already beginning to turn black. 'We came off cheap enough, lad—considering. There's blood on your face, but not from the blade of a knife. The rats! They couldn't make an honest fight of it. I was afraid for you when I saw that raw steel flash.'

Jeff said, cold anger still in him, 'That whelp will never draw another knife. I felt his skull give when I gun-whipped him. We left a dead man out there, Bill Ballinger.'

Ballinger shrugged his big shoulders. 'Had they their way they'd have left two dead men out there, you and me, Jeff Kennett. So why should we know any regret? Forget it. We'll wash up and I'll have our supper brought to this cabin, and while we eat we'll talk over this business you mentioned. I'm going to love you, Jeff Kennett. You're a fighting man after my own heart!'

★   ★   ★

A plentiful application of cold water cooled both Jeff's bruises and his anger and he ate enough to take the first edge from a gnawing hunger before squaring away with the business at hand.

'I've got two thousand head of Texas cattle up in the Lassen Meadows,' he said. 'I have a crew of riders holding the herd there to rest and fatten up, while I dicker for a means to transport the cattle to the San Francisco market, which, I understand, is hungry for beef. Transport of course, means by boat. So, I've come to you. Both taking the herd in by boat, and having you do the job, if possible, were suggestions from Dave Mowrie.'

Captain Bill whistled softly. 'Two thousand head, you say? Man! You've a fortune there. You wouldn't be telling me you brought that herd all the way from Texas?'

'All the way from Texas. They told me I was crazy when I started. Looking back over what the boys and I went through along the trail, maybe they were right. We've been two years on the trail.' A sombre note crept into Jeff's voice. 'All those who started the drive with me are not at Lassen Meadows,' he continued. 'We dug graves along that trail. Some we dug plenty deep, and drove the whole herd over them, so that no scalp-hunting Indian would find them and dig them up. We went through hell for weeks and months. We climbed mountains, we swam rivers, we crossed deserts. We hungered and thirsted. We froze and we sweltered. We fought Indians and we fought white renegades. But we got here.'

Jeff fell silent, staring at his plate. A great respect grew in Captain Bill's eyes as he studied the lean, grave face across the table from him and glimpsed in some part the terrific hardship and toil and danger that had ridden every step of those endless miles.

'That makes anything I ever did in my life look small and useless by comparison, Jeff Kennett,' Ballinger said quietly. 'Well, you didn't hesitate tonight when I needed help, so I won't hesitate now. We'll get that herd of yours to San Francisco, every head of it. And we'll get it there by boat, if we have to fight our way every mile along the river.'

Jeff's head came up quickly. 'Why should we have to fight our way? Why should anyone try and stop us?'

'Plenty of reasons why, lad. First off, this whole stretch of country is beef hungry. Whoever told you they wanted beef in San Francisco, and wanted it bad, wasn't lying to you. But they told only part of the story. Ain't a miner in the diggings who wouldn't give an ounce of gold dust for a haunch of beef, and he wouldn't give a tinker's damn who he bought it from, whether it was stolen or otherwise. They cleaned John Sutter of beef, early in the rush. They've worked on the Spanish herds until the dons have been forced to move what was left way back into the big central plains, where they keep crews of vaqueros on guard night and day. A rush of human beings like this country is seeing is like a swarm of locusts. They eat up everything in sight. Right now, if you were to go up town and try and buy a sack of flour it would cost you close to fifty dollars. Get further back into the diggings and you'd be lucky to get that sack for twice the amount. No, soon as the word gets out that you got two thousand head of beef cattle heading for San Francisco, you'll know what I mean when I say you'll have to fight your way through.'

Listening gravely, Jeff nodded. 'You said there were several reasons we'd have trouble moving the herd. That's only one of them. What are the others?'

Ballinger smiled grimly. 'You know what rammed into us this fine evening. It didn't just happen. That's how things are in the steamboat business along this river. That was Colonel Nathaniel Sharpe's and Captain Noah Carlin's way of fighting a rival concern—in this case the River Navigation Company, which owns this boat, the *Mother Lode*, and which pays my wages at present. Carlin was sore because I wouldn't let him bluff me out of a landing and, knowing he'd probably catch hell from Sharpe because he'd failed, he gathered up a gang of his bully boys and set out to get even. He probably would have if you hadn't cut in on my side. I owe you plenty, for that.'

Jeff waved a hand. 'I still can't see how anything of that sort can affect our moving cattle down river.'

The captain leaned forward. 'Here's the whole picture, in brief. Steamboat competition along this river has reached the dog eat dog stage. There are half a dozen big concerns operating anywhere from two to half a dozen boats. Then there are better than a dozen independent owners, skippering their own boats. The bigger operators are out to drive the little fellows off the river—complete. They've cut passenger and freight rates to a point that's ridiculous. Know what it cost that gang of gold hunters per head to ride with me up from San Francisco? One dollar per. Right now it takes just one thin dime to buy a ride between Marysville and this berth where we're tied up. It can't go on, of course, or everybody will go bust. But the big outfits figure they can outlast the little fellers, which they probably can.

'If word about you needing transportation for your cattle was to get out, you'd have a dozen boat owners clawing at your coat tails. You could get 'em bidding against each other for the business and probably beat the freight rates down to almost nothing. And then the fellow who got the business would start right in figuring how he could euchre you, to make his money back, even if he had to knock you on the head and throw you overboard and sell the cattle as his own. Oh, we got some pretty scoundrels sailing our fair river, and probably the prettiest of the crowd is Noah Carlin, with his partner, Nate Sharpe, not far behind. And mark what I say, whoever sets out to haul your cattle, will have every trick of the trade pulled on him before he gets a loaded boat down the river. So there it is, lad. But if you want me for the job, we'll get at it.'

Jeff Kennett studied the face of the man opposite. He marked the vigorous but graying thatch of hair, the square, fighting, weather beaten jaw and the level eyes which always seemed halfway between a twinkle and the lighting fires of a tumultuous temper.

'You're my man, of course,' he agreed. 'But you have a job now, skippering this boat.'

A deep laugh rumbled in Bill Ballinger's throat. 'It's an even bet I won't have, come morning. That petty larceny crew in the office are biting their nails because I came near scraping some paint off their nice new boat in driving Carlin out of this berth. By morning they'll be fit to tie, just thinking about it. So I wouldn't be surprised if I was told that the *Mother Lode* would be put under a more cautious man, from here on out. Oh, I know this river, lad—and the men along it.'

'But you couldn't haul cattle on the *Mother Lode* anyhow,' said Jeff.

'No. But I know a boat we can haul 'em on, and I'm sure we can charter it. It's old and not too fast, but it has sound engines in it and a staunch bottom, which is more than you can say of a lot of the tubs creaking up and down the tide. What say we go see about that charter?'

'I'm all for quick action,' nodded Jeff. 'But I still feel that you're doing this because you think you're under obligation to me just because I tied into that brawl on your side. And I don't want that.'

Captain Bill clapped a brawny hand on Jeff's shoulder. 'You're more than half wrong,' he chuckled. 'I'm doing this because I like the idea, because I see shoal water ahead and I like a job that calls for navigating shoal water. Come along!'

★   ★   ★

Crossing the gangplank to shore, they headed for the ragged line of yellow waterfront lights winking through the fog. Soon Captain Bill was leading the way into a rough boarded, two story building which carried the sign Jackson House above its doorway. This was a hotel, as Jeff saw by the guest register open on a rough counter, with a string of keys hanging from a row of nails on the wall beyond.

In one corner of the room, with a lamp at her elbow, sat a stout rosy-cheeked, jolly looking woman of middle age, busy at a lap full of knitting. She looked up, fixed them with a merry eye. 'You've been fighting again, Bill Ballinger. Or should I say—still? I live in hopes that the day will come when I'll see you without a black eye or a skinned up face. Don't you ever weary of it?'

Ballinger smiled. 'It is the breed of rats that infest this world, Lizzie. They just won't let me be. Lizzie, shake hands with my good friend, Jeff Kennett. Jeff, this is Lizzie Jackson, who might have married me if she hadn't liked the looks of that old river rat, Anse Jackson, better. It was a sad day for us both when he died, for he was a fine husband for Lizzie and like a brother to me. This river could use a few men like Anse Jackson, these days.'

The woman's hand was firm and warm and her quick eyes friendly. 'Shame on you, Bill Ballinger,' she accused. 'You've led this boy astray, I see. He's been fighting, too.'

Captain Bill whooped delightedly. 'Nary a bit of leading did he need, Lizzie. He barged in of his own account and a tiger cat he was. You should have seen him lay Noah Carlin low. It was a beautiful punch.'

Lizzie Jackson's face sobered. 'As if Noah Carlin and Nate Sharpe didn't hate you enough already. What did you do to stir them up this time?'

'I wouldn't let Carlin and that old scow, the *Gold Camp*, bluff me out of my berthing. It was deliberate on his part and when he couldn't get away with it, he laid for me with a gang of roughs. And that's how it happened, so you needn't lay such an accusing eye on me. But to business. Lizzie, I'd like to charter the old *Flame of Sunset* for a month or six weeks. Me and Jeff Kennett here have some business in mind.'

Lizzie Jackson pursed her generous lips and frowned slightly. 'I'd have to know the kind of business you've in mind, Bill Ballinger. I wouldn't put it past you to start river pirating, if you thought you could stir up some extra trouble that way. And Anse Jackson would turn over in his grave if you did anything to give his old boat a bad name. I say, what is this business?'

'Cattle, ma'am—taking cattle by boat to the San Francisco market,' said Jeff Kennett.

He went on to explain briefly of his herd and his plans for it. Lizzie Jackson followed his every word attentively, studying him all the while he was speaking. When he finished she said simply, 'Anse Jackson would have liked such a deal, himself. Yes, you can have the *Flame of Sunset*. But mark you, Bill Ballinger, you're to carry this out as peaceful as possible and not start an entire war along our river.'

'Lizzie darlin',' exclaimed Captain Bill, 'I give you my word. Only,' and here a twinkle came into his eye, 'I'd be lying if I didn't admit I'd be a mite disappointed if Nate Sharpe and Noah Carlin failed to try and put a snag or two in our course.'

CHAPTER FIVE

The *Flame of Sunset* was tied up in a backwater called South Slough, about a mile down river from town. She was a side wheeler and small, compared with the towering *Mother Lode*. But she had been built for cargo rather than passenger service in the first place, and her decks, fore and aft, Jeff Kennett figured, would, when properly bulwarked, hold upwards of two hundred head or better of Texas cattle. Jeff's knowledge of boats was meagre enough, but as Captain Bill Ballinger took him over the craft, pointing out this and that, Jeff saw they could hardly have found a craft more admirably suited to their purpose.

A thin and ancient Scot, Andy McLain, had been living aboard the boat as watchman and caretaker. In the old days when Anse Jackson had been alive and skippering the *Flame*, Andy McLain had been his engineer. When Captain Bill asked the old fellow about the condition of his engines Andy took them below and pointed with justifiable pride.

'Honest Scot engines they are,' twanged old Andy, 'better'n most on the river today. Been a heap of comfort to me, they have, keeping them clean and shined. For I've had the feeling always that there'd come a job of work for them to do again, one of these days.'

'And you were right, Andy,' rumbled Captain Bill. 'There is a job. How long before you can get up steam?'

Andy's faded eyes shone. 'Get me the proper help, Cap'n Bill, and it won't be long.'

'You'll have it,' the captain promised. 'Come this time tomorrow and the *Flame of Sunset* will be berthed alongside of Thompson's lumber yard. On the way up we'll rasp her bottom across a sand bar or two to clean off the moss. And then, after a bit of timber work, we'll be ready for the job. I'll be back this afternoon with crew enough to get her moving, Andy.'

Back in town, Captain Bill bustled off to line up a crew, leaving Jeff Kennett to his own devices. A visit to one of the stores and to a tawdry barber shop next door, bought him a fresh outfit of clothes, a comforting shave and a trim clipping of his long, tawny hair. The prices were steep, but Jeff paid without complaint. The clothes he carried to the *Mother Lode*, where, in Captain Bill's cabin, he washed and changed. His old, ragged trail-stained outfit he consigned to the river waters and when he again went ashore, he had the feeling of being a new man in a new world.

To Jeff's relief, the hovering fog had now lifted and vanished. He remembered the horse he had left in Tom Hankins' care at the stage station and bent his steps that way. Before he reached it, however, he saw a familiar gleaming carriage and fretting, spirited team standing before a big trading post building. In the carriage sat a slim, familiar figure, features demurely shadowed by a dainty poke-bonnet. Jeff's pulse quickened, and almost before he realized it, he had crossed to the side of the carriage. He lifted his hat and said, 'It's good to see you again, and in sunlight, Miss Deborah Sharpe. I hope you've recovered from the unpleasant moments of yesterday.'

She looked down at him, a faintly dawning smile on her lips. 'I've quite recovered, thank you, Jeff Kennett,' she answered.

'And—er—Aunt Amanda?' questioned Jeff.

Her laugh was quick and full of music. 'Also quite well, I assure you. And happy to have proof of her contention that the limit of civilization is less than a mile from Boston.'

After this momentary exchange of words they fell silent, and as their stillness grew and mutual regard lengthened the moment rose intangibly taut with a strange and quickening emotion, an emotion which softened the clear, silver gray of Jeff Kennett's eyes, and sent waves of warm color across the girl's cheeks. Jeff moved a step closer.

'Deborah,' he said softly—'you're lovely!'

Her head dropped forward until the poke bonnet hid all but the flawless curve of her chin and the faint sweet smile on her lips.

'You mustn't, Jeff Kennett,' she murmured. 'You mustn't look at me, speak to me—that way. You don't—understand. But—you mustn't.'

The tide of warm, rich fire was flooding all through Jeff Kennett now and, despite her low protest, he would have said more. But the magic moment was broken into by the sound of imperative footsteps. A voice, curt and brusque, said, 'Introduce me to your friend, Deborah. I do not believe I have met him before.'

Jeff turned. Here stood a rawboned, burly figure of a man, in the uniform of a steamboat captain. On the left side of his face, running from the angle of his jaw up to under the eye, was a deep and savage bruise, still puffed and swollen. And Jeff remembered immediately that brawl of the night before, remembered the figure that had come charging in from the side, and the single devastating punch he had landed in the face of that man.

The girl was speaking, her voice low and troubled. 'Jeff Kennett, meet Captain Noah Carlin. Noah, this is the rider who was so kind to Aunt Amanda and me at that stage holdup, yesterday.'

It was instinct, perhaps, which told Noah Carlin who Jeff was, for it was not probable that in the hurly burly of the night before, in the fog and darkness, he had caught any clear look at Jeff before Jeff's punch had put him out of the fight completely. But by the sudden fury which burned in his eyes he advertised the fact that he knew Jeff all right. So Jeff said, a bite of mockery in his voice, 'We've met before, Captain Carlin and I, Miss Sharpe. Under conditions not nearly so pleasant.'

Carlin took a half step toward Jeff, his fists clenched, his predatory mouth white and knotted. 'I wouldn't presume too far, Kennett—on an accident.'

Jeff shrugged. 'No accident. I hit what I aimed at. I think you'll agree I really hit.'

Carlin was fairly trembling with rage. Here, Jeff thought, was a vain man, to whom defeat of any kind was a galling gnawing thing, a man who could be dangerous and implacable in his hatred.

The girl, wide eyed and startled, was looking from one to the other of the two men, trying to gauge the cause for this display of animosity. Half formed words were on her lips, but Noah Carlin gave her no chance to utter them.

'We'll meet again, Kennett,' he said with a grinding effort at self control. Then he climbed into the carriage beside the girl and growled an order to the liveried coachman. As the carriage rolled swiftly away, Jeff Kennett was conscious of the girl's eyes fixed on him, vastly troubled and regretful.

★ ★ ★

They brought the *Flame of Sunset* out of South Slough and up river to the berthing Captain Bill Ballinger had selected. Then with stout timbers carried down from Thompson's lumber yard they set about bulwarking the cargo decks into cattle pens. The little crew Captain Bill had rounded up were mostly older men, men who had traveled the river under him, friends of old standing and who possessed in some degree his spirit of rough and ready independence and aggressiveness. Under Captain Bill's directions they sawed and fitted and spiked the heavy timbers into place. A score of Chinese coolie laborers filed back and forth from shore to boat, carrying lengths of cordwood to stoke the fires under the boilers. And Andy McLain fussed endlessly with his beloved engines.

This show of outfitting and industry attracted the attention of a number of river front loafers who argued and speculated on the why and how of these preparations. Questions were shouted at the toiling crew and Captain Bill set off a gale of uproarious laughter when he explained, with perfectly straight face, that they were preparing to go to the South Seas after a load of ring tailed baboons.

A fussy, choleric looking little man in dandified dress appeared, and picked his way through the crowd of loafers and across the gangplank. He accosted Captain Bill shrilly. Was he, or wasn't he, the little man demanded, prepared to skipper the *Mother Lode* back to San Francisco, starting at four o'clock that afternoon?

Captain Bill answered by picking the little man up bodily and holding him dangling over the amber, sliding river water. The little man kicked and squealed in fright, while the watchers whooped. Then Captain Bill set the little man back on the gangplank, gave him a spank and the advice to run along and not bother him any more. Safely back on the bank, the little man fairly danced with rage, shrilling the information that Captain Bill was discharged and that he would be blacklisted all up and down the river. To all of which Captain Bill merely gave a mocking wave and went back to work.

Jeff Kennett, spectator to this, said, 'Listen, Bill. You're giving up too much. I can't have you do this. It might mean your future career.'

The captain chuckled. 'Don't worry, lad. That old fuss-budget couldn't blacklist anybody, least of all Bill Ballinger. You see, I happen to know that Lucien Field, that's yonder noisy little man, and the rest of his like in the River Transportation Company, have been combing all Sacramento for a man to take my place. Didn't I tell you that the more they thought about that little brush I had with Noah Carlin and the *Gold Camp*, the more jittery they would become? So they've been looking for another skipper for the *Mother Lode*, and haven't been able to uncover one. Now they've come back to me. Well, devil take them! The *Mother Lode* can lay at her berthing forever, for all of me. I got better business ahead.'

Along toward the middle of the afternoon, a pale, mousy looking man accosted Jeff Kennett as Jeff stepped ashore for a moment. He handed over a sealed envelope with an unintelligible murmur of comment, then

hurried away before Jeff could say anything.
The envelope carried Jeff's name written in bold, dashing pen strokes. Jeff opened the envelope, drew out the enclosure and read:

Jefferson Kennett, Esq.

I would appreciate your presence as my guest at dinner this evening at seven o'clock, that I may more fully express my thanks and appreciation for the kindness and protection you rendered my daughter and my sister during the unpleasant conditions surrounding that attempted stage holdup.

Respectfully,
Nathaniel Sharpe

This was the last thing in the world Jeff had expected. He read the epistle a second time, then crossed back to the *Flame of Sunset* and drew Bill Ballinger aside.

'Read this, Bill,' he said, 'and tell me what you think of it.'

Captain Bill read, then pushed a big hand through his graying thatch. 'I don't want to hurt your feelings, lad. Knowing Nate Sharpe, and I know him well, I can't feel that he means what he says here, at all.'

Jeff nodded grimly. 'My own reaction, Bill, from the impression I had of him. What you're driving at is that, while he may want to see me, his real purpose is something other than what he claims?'

'Exactly! He's wondering what we're up to, Nate Sharpe is, wondering why we're bringing the old *Flame of Sunset* back to life, why we're fixing her up this way. He's shrewd enough to have maybe guessed something of the truth, but he'd like to know more. Ay! Nate Sharpe is up to something.'

'Then you think I'd best pay no attention?'

'Not at all! Take him up, lad. You go there and find out all you can of what he has under his hat. Whatever you find out can't hurt us, while it may help. Ay, you go there, and show him you can play as shrewd a poker hand as he can.'

Both Jeff and Captain Bill had brought their personal gear aboard the *Flame of Sunset*. That evening, in the little cabin they shared together, Captain Bill watched Jeff prepare for his visit to Colonel Sharpe's home. He saw Jeff unearth a sheer silk neckerchief from his pack and knot it about his brown, corded throat, and his eyes twinkled. 'I've observed the lass several times, lad—and she is a bright and lovely thing. The wonder of it is that Nate Sharpe could father such a fine girl.'

Jeff had stripped off his belted guns, but now he drew one of them from its holster and slipped the weapon down inside the waist band of his trousers, well around to one side, where the flap of his beaded buckskin vest hid it. To this, Captain Bill nodded grave approval.

'I've no worries now that Nate Sharpe will get the best of you in any way,' he said. 'You're a lad of rare foresight. The house, and the finest it is in all the town, stands near the head of K Street among some grand great oaks. I'll be waiting up to hear about it all.'

Considering the time and place the home of Colonel Nathaniel Sharpe was sumptuous in its furnishings. Jeff thought, with a certain grim irony, of the strange surroundings a man might find himself in, along new and far trails. Only short weeks ago he had been battling mocking desert and eating his meals beside a campfire from battered, smoke-blackened utensils. Now, he was sitting down to a table of spotless linen, gleaming glass and chinaware. Truly, this was Eldorado, the land of fabled magic. And magic indeed was the slim figure of Deborah across the table from him.

At first things were somewhat stilted. Then Colonel Sharpe, at the end of the table to Jeff's left, began conversing easily and Jeff answered in kind, weighing and studying this man so impeccably groomed, so ramrod straight in physical carriage. The man was handsome and, at first glance, looked masterful. But closer scrutiny of the mouth above the goatee showed a faint weakness in line and the flashing eyes were so restless they gave Jeff the impression of a vague shiftiness. But the man was smooth—and into his conversation he deftly slid a question to which Jeff was nodding assent before he realized the commitment.

'I suppose you, as a newly arrived cattleman, are connected with that herd I understand is being held in Lassen Meadows?'

Jeff, realizing that his unconscious nod already answered the question in the affirmative, said, 'Yes, that's right. I own it.'

'Indeed! You brought the herd across the plains?'

'From Texas,' said Jeff.

It was Aunt Amanda's turn to exclaim. 'Gracious! Isn't that an awful long way, young man?'

Jeff smiled slightly. 'Quite a long way, yes, ma'am.'

'Why, it must have taken you months!'

'Two years,' Jeff told her.

'My sakes alive! Two years! Didn't the Indians bother you?'

'They bothered us—some,' Jeff admitted.

In its very brevity, Jeff's answer told more of what that long trail had been like than a flood of words could have. Aunt Amanda looked at him keenly.

'Do you know, you are a rather remarkable young man?' she said. 'Remarkable!'

Colonel Nathaniel Sharpe said smoothly, 'An achievement—a real achievement.'

The meal concluded, Colonel Sharpe led the way to a room of easy lounging chairs and books, with buffalo robes for rugs and a gun case along an inner wall. A second door was framed on the far side of the room. The women did not accompany them and Jeff, throwing a last glance at Deborah Sharpe, was startled at the look he saw on her face. It was a troubled look, tinged with worry, almost warning.

Colonel Sharpe closed the door, held out a box of cigars to Jeff, selected one himself. He said abruptly, 'I am interested in that herd of yours, Kennett, and what disposition you plan for it.'

'Yes?' drawled Jeff.

The older man frowned through a cloud of tobacco smoke. 'Yes. You are considering marketing it as beef, in San Francisco, perhaps?'

'Perhaps,' said Jeff.

A faint tinge of color ran through Colonel Sharpe's cheeks. 'Suppose we quit fencing and get down to business,' he said curtly. 'The *Flame of Sunset* is being bulwarked and prepared to transport cattle. The obvious market for those cattle is San Francisco. That is freight business and my company is interested in freight business. We are prepared to haul your cattle at a lower rate than any other transportation concern along the river. Just what rate is Ballinger offering you? We'll give you a better deal, whatever it is.'

Jeff's eyes narrowed and he smiled faintly. 'I'm satisfied with the setup as is, Colonel. Sorry.'

The colonel snorted. 'Nonsense! You brought that herd into California to realize as much profit as possible on it. Every dollar you can save is just that much more in your pocket.'

'I'm still satisfied,' murmured Jeff.

Colonel Sharpe took a short turn up and down the room. 'What do you know about Ballinger? Have you any idea of that man's record?'

'I take people as I find them,' said Jeff. 'And Captain Bill Ballinger rates as quite a man in my book. I like him.'

The colonel waved an impatient hand. 'I could tell you things about that man—I could tell you things—! But another point. That boat, the *Flame of Sunset*—why, there isn't a rottener bottom on the river. The boilers are thin, the engines worn out. Just a creaking old hulk, all the way through. I wouldn't trust a load of river gravel to it, let alone a herd of valuable cattle. Every boat my company operates is a good boat, a sound boat, a fast boat. Your cattle will be safe with us and we will haul them cheaper than anyone else. Come, man—come! You can't be foolish enough to overlook all those advantages.'

Colonel Sharpe, who had been pacing restlessly, stopped to stare down at Jeff. Meeting the stare, Jeff saw the colonel's eyes take on that faint shiftiness. In sudden disgust he said curtly, 'There's no use of further argument. I've made my plans. Captain Bill Ballinger and the *Flame of Sunset* carry my cattle.'

A tide of angry colour whipped through the colonel's cheeks again. 'That is your last word, Kennett?'

'My last word.'

'We'll see!' snapped Colonel Sharpe.

He turned to the inner door, jerked it open. Two men stepped through it into the room. One of them was Captain Noah Carlin. The other was a thick set, black browed individual, with hard, black eyes.

Jeff came swiftly to his feet. He said nothing, but his eyes were icy. Colonel Sharpe said, 'The man's a fool, as I feared, Noah. See what you can do with him.'

Captain Noah Carlin looked at Jeff, sneering. He said, 'You have a final chance to change your mind, Kennett. You'll deal with us, or you'll never see a single head of your cattle reach the San Francisco market. Well?'

'Never,' said Jeff, 'is a long, long time.

And I'd see every head of my herd dead and eaten by honest buzzards than to let a flock of crooked, human ones have anything to do with them. Sharpe, how can you live with yourself, posing as a gentleman?'

Colonel Sharpe's face went livid, but the furious words which seethed in him died in his throat. 'I'm leaving,' said Jeff coldly. 'Can't stand the company.'

'Not so fast!' rapped Captain Noah Carlin. 'A little matter for you to settle with the civil authorities first, Kennett. The matter of a dead man. A man you killed. Murdered is perhaps the correct word. A most brutal thing, I must say. You crushed his skull with the barrel of a gun. I happened to be witness to it.'

The old, cold fires stirred through Jeff Kennett, and there was danger in his laugh.

'Won't work, Carlin,' he said. 'It won't work at all. Least of all your claim to being witness. At the time that whelp drew a knife and I gunwhipped him before he could use it, you weren't witnessing anything. Because, just before that you had run into something—something which put you out of the fight complete. Your face still shows what happened to you, and you wanted no more of it, did you, Carlin? Once was enough—a big plenty. So, you left it up to your hired thugs to finish the job, and they couldn't do it, even if one of them did pull a knife. This bluff won't work any better than the one you tried on Bill Ballinger to keep him from berthing the *Mother Lode*. You can't scare me, Carlin—you aren't man enough to carry through.'

The scorching mockery of Jeff's words filled Noah Carlin with a shaking rage. He jerked around towards the thick set, black browed man who had accompanied him into the room.

'Marshal Taggart, arrest that man! The charge is murder, and I will swear to it. Arrest him!'

Taggart nodded and started forward, but stopped dead still, half through a stride. Jeff Kennett's hand had flicked under the flap of his vest. As it came into view again, it cradled a heavy Colt gun, the muzzle of which took in the three men before him in a steady arc.

'No!' said Jeff. 'There'll be nothing like that. I wondered what was the real purpose behind your invitation, Sharpe. I did not think it would be quite this bad, but I came prepared. Reach—the three of you! Reach high!'

Colonel Nathaniel Sharpe gave a queer, blurting grasp and his arms jerked upwards swiftly. Captain Noah Carlin's hands lifted a trifle more slowly, but they lifted. Taggart, with a resigned shrug, followed suit.

Jeff backed to the door. 'You'll stay right

here for a good ten minutes after I've gone. You'll do that if you want to keep whole skins. I fought a lot more men than you three, along that trail from Texas. Red men, most of them—but better men than you. I didn't let them stop me, and I can't see you making good where they couldn't. This isn't a bluff, Carlin. This is cold turkey. Don't try and follow me—any of you!'

Colonel Sharpe and Taggart said nothing, but Noah Carlin, his lips twisted in helpless fury, blurted, 'You'll never get that herd down river, Kennett. You'll see. You'll never get it down river!'

'Words, Carlin. Just words,' mocked Jeff. 'I still say, never is a long, long time. Good evening, gentlemen!'

Jeff reached his free hand behind him, opened the door and backed through. He closed the door and went swiftly out of the house, seeing no one along the way. Outside the night was clear and crisp, the stars bright. Jeff put away his gun, headed off through the grove of oaks. The air seemed strangely clean and good to his nostrils, cooling the fires of anger still running through him.

Then he heard his name called, very softly and hesitantly. He turned and saw her standing beside the wide bole of a towering oak. She was just a pale blur in the darkness.

Harsh words were on Jeff's lips, but he held them back and stood there, saying nothing. She came over to him, stood before him. 'You didn't—do business with them, did you, Jeff? You didn't agree—to anything? Because you mustn't. You can't trust them, Jeff—not even my father.'

She was wringing her slim hands. Jeff, seeking for an answer to this astounding setup, could find none for a moment. 'I should have warned you,' she stammered. 'I—I wanted to, Jeff. But I had no chance—no chance to talk to you before—'

Jeff's hands went out, caught her by the shoulders. He shook her gently. 'I don't understand this, Deborah Sharpe—I don't understand it at all. But—I did not do business with them, and I'm not going to, if that will make you feel better.'

She gave a little sob, but it was of relief, and her head came up. 'I'm glad, Jeff—oh, so glad. But you must be careful. I heard them talking, figuring what your herd would be worth, in San Francisco, even here, to sell to the miners. And they mean to have that herd—if they can.'

'They?' questioned Jeff.

'Noah Carlin and—my father.' It was as though she had been hit with a whip. Her head dropped again and she whispered, 'What you must think of me—think of me—'

Jeff drew her a little closer, cupped a finger under her soft chin, lifted her bent head. 'I think you're a thoroughbred, Deborah

Sharpe. I think—I know, I'll never forget you.'

It might have been the trickery of the starlight, filtering down through the oaks, but it seemed that she was leaning toward him, her face lifting. Then somehow she was in his arms, the warm, sweet magic of her lips against his own. A moment later she had slipped away and was running, light as a moonbeam, back through the oaks toward the house.

CHAPTER SIX

As he made his way back toward the moiling riverfront, Jeff Kennett found himself wondering if this night had been real, if it wasn't all some part of a crazy dream. It was difficult to reconcile the fact that a girl like Deborah Sharpe was of the same flesh and blood as that evasive, tricky individual, Colonel Nathanial Sharpe. But it must have been real, for the warm sweetness of her lips seemed still to linger on his own, and the soft music of her voice still in his ears.

Jeff shook his head, clearing his thoughts and fixing his eyes in front of him. It seemed to him that the reflected glow of light from the riverfront was inordinately bright. There was, as he looked closer, a focal point to that glare. Were his eyes tricking him, he wondered, or did he see a crimson tinted roll of smoke, lifting upward against the dark?

In ten more steps, Jeff Kennett was running.

'Fire! Fire!' came the shout from the crowd. 'The *Flame of Sunset*! Fire!'

A wildly milling, shouting, excited mob lined the river bank, most of them sober, a few drunk. Jeff Kennett fought his way through the crush, paying no attention to the angry growls and curses of those he ruthlessly pushed out of his way. He broke into the clear, almost falling over a chattering Chinese coolie.

The *Flame of Sunset* was burning—there was no doubt of that. But the fire seemed all on the forward cargo deck, and there were men fighting it. Through the belching smoke Jeff made out the looming figure of Captain Bill Ballinger and Bill's big voice roared orders above the crackle of the flames.

Jeff raced across the gangplank and dropped down to the deck. Captain Bill and his little crew were fighting valiantly, scooping up river water with buckets on the end of ropes and sloshing the contents across the flames. One of the men, half coughing and gulping from the smoke, was momentarily done in. Jeff pulled him aside, grabbed his bucket and joined the others. Within a minute or two he saw that the fire was not gaining any headway, but in fact was being driven back.

A roar of triumph broke from Bill Ballinger. 'Stay with it, boys—stay with it! We're holding it, and Andy is rigging a hose. We'll lick it. More water!'

Jeff scooped up water, flung it across the flames, scooped up more. Smoke burned his eyes, stung his throat and lungs, and it seemed as if he could feel the skin of his face crawl from the heat. But he fought doggedly on, losing all count of how many buckets of water he hoisted across the rail. Then out of a hatchway came two men, dragging a hose between them. Almost immediately the hose writhed and fattened and a pounding stream of water slashed across the very heart of the flames.

Bill Ballinger yelled, 'That's it, boys! We got it now!'

Jeff dropped his bucket, moved back, gulping hungrily at clearer air. A raucous yell sounded on the bank.

'They can't stop that fire—they can't stop it! And with the boat going up, it might start a fire that'll take the whole town. Cut the mooring lines! Let the river drift that boat out of here. Cut the mooring lines!'

Jeff Kennett knew crowds, and how senseless they could become in a panic brought on by real or fancied danger. He whirled and went back across the gangplank at a run. Already there was a swaying of the crowd toward the tree stump about which was wound the forward mooring line. Some one was yelling, 'Get an ax! Somebody get an ax!'

Again Jeff fought through a jostling press of bodies. Again he was cursed and even struck at by those he tossed out of his way. When one of them, burly and combative, grabbed him roughly, Jeff smashed his fist into the fellow's jaw and drove on.

He reached the mooring stump just in time, for a lank, wild eyed fellow was already waving an ax and yelling for room to swing it. But he broke off abruptly when he found himself looking into the muzzle of Jeff's gun.

'Drop it!' rapped Jeff. 'Drop that ax! Quick!'

The ax dropped and so did the fellow's chin. He backed up hurriedly, along with the rest. Jeff turned on them with cold anger.

'You crazy fools! Can't you see that fire's under control—that there's no further danger? Where's the man who started this idea of cutting the *Flame of Sunset* loose? Where is he?'

This was a question no one seemed able to answer, nor did the author of that first bawl of panic step forward to advertise himself. Jeff picked up the ax and tossed it in the river. His gun waved a threatening arc.

'Get away from this mooring line—all of

you. Get plenty away! I'll shoot any man who tries to cut this line!'

Now Bill Ballinger came rushing up. He was dripping wet, singed and smoke-blackened and seething with anger.

'Good boy, Jeff!' he panted. 'Don't fool with 'em a minute. Blow down the first one who makes a move. I've had a big bellyful of crooked work this night and I'm ready to hurt somebody—bad! That line all right?'

'All right, Bill. How about the stern line?'

'Safe. Harry Travers, gambler friend of mine, is watching that. Harry's looking at the fools over a derringer.'

By this time it was plain to all that the fire was whipped. Water from the fire hose had beaten the flames to fragments and was now sluicing out these fragments, one by one. Soon the last of these was gone and only acrid steam rose from the scorched and charred deck. The crowd broke up and began filtering away toward the beckoning lights of the waterfront dives.

Bill Ballinger put guards over each of the mooring stumps then said to Jeff, 'Come on. Want to show you something.'

He led the way aboard and into the crew's cabin. There, on the deck, lay the body of a man. Captain Bill nudged the figure with his toe.

'I hit him pretty hard. Hope I didn't break his neck. But I was kind of wild eyed about then and in a hell of a hurry. I wanted to make sure he'd stay put until I got ready to ask him some questions.' He gave the figure a harder nudge with his boot and the figure groaned and stirred. 'Thought so,' he grunted. 'His kind is too damned low and worthless to kill easy. That's the one who started the fire, Jeff. He sneaked aboard, sluiced a bucket of whale oil across the for'd cargo deck and touched it off with a bundle of greasy waste, which he lit and tossed into the oil. I saw him, just as he threw that waste. He made a run for it, but I caught him just as he reached the shore. I slugged him and dragged him back and threw him in here. Then I went to fightin' fire. Man! It was warm work there for a little while.'

'How much damage do you think, Bill?'

'Dunno, for sure. Not too much, I hope. I'll have Andy look it over soon as things cool down a bit. Don't believe it got through the deck. But had it got a couple of minutes start we'd be minus a boat, right now.'

A figure appeared in the doorway, a figure in the long dark coat of a gambler. The newcomer said in a quiet, almost colorless voice, 'Just wanted to know if everything was all right, Bill.'

'Sure, Harry—sure. Everything's fine. Come on in and shake hands with Jeff Kennett. Jeff, this is Harry Travers, a 'square' gambler. Glad you dropped in,

Harry. This swab on the floor is the one who started the fire and, while I ain't had too good a look at him, I'm sort of sure I've never seen him before. Maybe you have. Let's get him up here where we can look at him.'

Bill bent over, locked one huge hand on the fellow's shoulder and lifted him erect with the same ease he would a child. The fellow's features were slack, his eyes stupid and dazed. Bill pulled him over to a light and stared at him, then shook his head. 'Can't recall him.'

'I can,' murmured Harry Travers. 'Not his name, but I've seen him before. He was in the Eagle this afternoon, drinking with Shag Taggart.'

'Ah!' rumbled Bill. 'And Shag Taggart is one of Noah Carlin's pet poodles. Might have known. Looks like the man we can really thank for our little fire is Captain Noah Carlin. That bucko gets rougher all the time. Jeff, what'll we do with this swab?'

'No percentage in doing anything with him, now,' said Jeff. 'I doubt he'll bother us again.'

'I'll cool him off a little, anyhow,' declared Bill.

He shoved the fellow out on shambling feet. At the rail Bill grabbed him, lifted him bodily and dropped him overside. There was a splash, a sputter of curses, a thrashing of water, then a sodden, dripping figure climbed up the dark bank, to slink rapidly away.

Jeff Kennett and Captain Bill Ballinger sat up late that night, talking. Jeff told all that had happened on his visit to the Sharpe home—all except the final few moments under the oaks.

Bill listened attentively. 'I ain't surprised,' he nodded finally. 'I knew Nate Sharpe was up to no good when he sent you that invite. And I ain't surprised they tried to put the screws on you when you turned them down flat. But they had a long nerve in trying to pass Shag Taggart off as a law officer, fit to arrest you or any other man. Shows how bad they would like to get their hands on the cattle. Wonder how they got to know about your herd?'

Jeff shrugged. 'Word travels and gets around here, I suppose, same as any other place. But that's beside the point. One fact is plain—the quicker we get started, the better. As long as we tie up here, Carlin and Sharpe will be figuring ways and means to work on us. And—we've been pretty lucky, so far.'

'Right you are,' Bill agreed. 'There'll have to be some new deck planks laid, but the beams underneath are sound enough. We can make that repair on our way up river. So, soon as we can get a load of planking aboard tomorrow morning, we cast off.' He stretched his big arms, yawned and grinned. 'How do you like our river and folks along it, lad?'

Jeff grinned back at him. 'The river is all right, but not all the folks. I'm lucky that I found one of the best of them.'

Bill reddened slightly. 'Just a damned old fool without sense enough to stay away from trouble,' he grunted. 'What say we turn in?'

Jeff lay awake in his bunk for some time, long after Bill Ballinger was snoring. His thoughts ran over all the night's happenings again and again, but each time came to pause at the memory of the soft oval of a face in the star spangled shelter of the oaks, and of the lingering sweetness of the lips that had pressed his. It was that thought that was with him as he finally fell asleep. But it seemed, dim in the night, just as sleep carried him off, that he heard the sound of a pistol shot, muffled with distance.

★   ★   ★

In the dawn light they made a new survey of the damage caused by the fire. Andy McLain already had a couple of the crew ripping up the charred and blackened planks, and he made a quick estimate of what was needed to replace them. He gave this to Captain Bill, who headed for the lumber yard. Jeff Kennett went up to the stage station to get his cow pony and was told that Tom Hankins was back in the stable somewhere.

But the person he bumped into in the stable was not Hankins. It was Harry Travers. The gambler, more quiet and inscrutable than ever, said gravely, 'How's chances for a ride up river as far as Red Bluff, Kennett?'

'Of course,' Jeff replied. 'Glad to have you, Travers. Soon as I collect my horse, we'll get down to the *Flame of Sunset.*'

Travers said, 'I'd better try and make it alone. They're still looking for me, and I don't want to drag you into it. If I can get aboard without them knowing it—'

Jeff looked at him keenly. 'They—looking for you? What's up, man?'

Travers shrugged. 'Last night. That fellow who started the fire, and who I identified as being a friend of Shag Taggart's? Well, he showed up at the Eagle, where I've been dealing—he and Taggart. They started rawhiding me. I tried to keep clear of them, but this fellow would have it. He forced it to a shoot out, and I downed him. Taggart stirred up a crowd and they spent most of the night hunting for me—with a rope. They never thought to look for me in this stable, but they are probably out on the prowl again this morning. So, I'll make my try for the boat, alone.'

Jeff frowned thoughtfully. So he had really

heard a shot last night, just before he fell asleep. And this was Harry Travers, a friend of Captain Bill's, who had been guarding the after mooring line of the boat.

'Wait a minute,' he said. 'I got an idea.'

He found Tom Hankins out back, explained tersely. Hankins said, 'Sure. There's some old clothes around. I'll get 'em for you, Kennett.'

Fifteen minutes later a raggedly clothed roustabout left the stage station, leading Jeff Kennett's pony, heading for the river front. And a little later Jeff himself, carrying a couple of bundles, went the same way. Presently, roustabout and horse were at the river bank and there Jeff joined them. 'You walked right past a gang of them, Harry,' he said softly. 'I heard your name mentioned, but not one of them gave you a second glance.'

Travers smiled at Jeff. 'The dumb can be blind, too.'

They had to blindfold the horse to get it across the gangplank and onto the boat, but it was safely done and presently a creaking wagon brought up the fresh planks from the lumber yard. These were quickly loaded. Five minutes later paddle wheels began to churn, and the *Flame of Sunset* nosed out into the river.

Up in the pilot house, Captain Bill nursed the wheel with one hand and with the other sent a mocking blast of the whistle echoing. But there was no sign of activity ashore and Bill turned to Jeff, standing beside him.

'Quiet,' he growled. 'Too damned quiet. We'd be fools to think that Carlin and Sharpe have given up. There's more deviltry cooking. I can feel it in my bones.'

CHAPTER SEVEN

Jeff Kennett found himself enjoying his first trip on the river immensely, for with each sweeping bend new vistas of beauty opened up. Wild life abounded. Ducks and wild fowl of all kinds swam in the still backwaters, or perched on sand and gravel bars. In the brush thickets deer scampered and in one bit of swamp land a herd of tule elk grazed. In a small pot hole beyond an eddy, Jeff saw a bear wallowing.

They saw men, also—searching the gravel bars of the main river with pick and pan and rocker. Most of these paid the *Flame of Sunset* little attention, except to shout a curse and shake a fist when the wash of her passing sent a wave surging along the gravel bars.

Captain Bill jerked his head towards a group of miners. 'No man so crazy as one gone gold crazy,' he said sententiously. 'I've hauled hundreds along this river, going and coming. They eat, drink, sleep and dream of nothing but gold—gold. Few of 'em profit much from what they get of it—they generally end up by losing it to smarter men.'

Jeff marveled at Ballinger's knowledge of this great tawny waterway, and at the unerring mastery with which he picked a deeper channel, avoiding hidden sand bar and waiting snag. At times, deep down in the engine room, he slowed the *Flame of Sunset* until she was barely moving, seeming almost to be feeling his way across some especially tricky stretch of water. Then again for long stretches he would send her thrashing full speed ahead, steadying the wheel with his foot, while he loaded and lighted and puffed vigorously on a black, stubby pipe. Meanwhile, down on the forward cargo deck, saws whined and hammers pounded. A growing patch of new, white lumber replaced the blackened, charred area where the fire had burned.

Gradually the river narrowed as the miles drifted backward. Their pace grew slower now, for here they had a stiffer current to drive against. Navigation too, grew more difficult. Several times, despite Captain Bill's wizardy at the wheel, they grounded on hidden sand and gravel bar, but each time, with a furious thrashing of paddle wheels, the *Flame of Sunset* drove valiantly clear and went staunchly on. And then, one afternoon a final curving sweep showed a lofty bank of reddish earth ahead. Atop that bank, on the west side of the river, was a huddle of buildings.

'Red Bluff,' said Captain Bill. 'Lassen Meadows are just about due east of here. You can go get your herd, Jeff.'

They tied up at the east bank, between the bank proper and the point of a gravel bar which angled down from above. 'Perfect place to load,' enthused Captain Bill. 'I'll have the boys build a good, heavy gangplank that will reach up from the bar. You can bring the cattle down the bar and the water on both sides will keep 'em pointed right. When you aiming to start, lad?'

'Right away,' said Jeff. 'The boys have had a long wait. I'll be seeing you, Bill.'

Jeff saddled his horse, led it ashore and swung into the saddle. He lifted a long arm in salute and struck east into the foothills. The horse was fresh and rested and Jeff was eager, so he rode the rest of the afternoon and through the night and greeted the next day's sun in country he remembered from his trip out. All through that day he pushed on, sticking to the backbone of a timbered ridge that thrust ever deeper into the climbing wilderness. Finally, in the smoky blue shadows of another dusk, Jeff broke from the timber into a vast meadow, where a camp fire winked, and the smell of cattle was in the air.

Jeff sent a Texas yell pealing, and was answered in kind. He spurred his weary bronc to a run and bore down upon the fire. Soon he was being joyously mauled by his faithful companions of the longest trail drive in the history of the west.

They plied Jeff with food and questions and listened avidly to all he had to tell. It was late before Jeff had a chance to ask a question himself. 'Any trouble since I left, Buck?'

Buck Yarnell shook his head. 'None to speak of. Oh, we've seen a few Injuns, but they ain't like some we met up with along the way. What trouble we've had has been with four legged varmits, wolves and a bear or two. But the boys laid a little lead here and there and the varmits got the idea, right peart. Never saw cattle go after grass like this herd has. Finest graze I ever saw. You can just watch the critters fat up. Where do we go from here, Jeff?'

'West to the big river. The boat is waiting for us. Come tomorrow we'll cut out about three hundred head for a quick drive. The rest of the herd will follow at a slower gait, as we can only take so many at a time on the boat. But them we can't take will be drifted south along the river meadows, feeding as they go, and each time as we come back with the boat for another load, we'll have less distance to cover.'

*   *   *

By noon of the next day the smaller herd was well on its way, with the balance of the cattle following at a more leisurely rate. Jeff took Buck and a couple of other hands with him to drive the smaller herd, and with the cattle full fed and rested, they pushed them hard.

Jeff had had a last word with Stony Peters, whom he'd left in charge of the main herd. 'From this and that which took place down river, Stony—putting the herd through to San Francisco isn't going to be a Sunday parade. This whole country is beef hungry and this herd is worth more money out here than any herd the same size ever was before. It represents an easier way of making money than digging it out of a gulch. We can expect trouble anywhere and any time, from here on out. So watch yourself and don't hesitate about laying a little lead where it will do the most good, if anybody comes bothering. For there is no more law out here than there was in the wildest desert we came across.'

Stony, tall and gaunt and still faced, nodded. 'Me and the boys didn't help bring that herd this far to lose it here. Don't you worry none, Jeff.'

It took two full days of hard driving to get the advance herd to the river, and they arrived in the evening, too late to load. So the cattle were held in a little river meadow, where they were glad to rest and feed.

There was a banging and clattering of hammers on the river side of the *Flame of Sunset* and when Jeff looked over there he was surprised to see a broad, squat barge moored there. Men of the *Flame of Sunset*'s crew were making the best of the last daylight as they put the finishing touches on a stout railing around the barge.

'Where'd that come from?' asked Jeff.

Captain Bill grinned. 'Harry Travers won it in a poker game over yonder in town.' He jerked his head towards the buildings of Red Bluff.

'Poker game! How—?'

The gambler, standing nearby, nodded. 'Bill and I went over to town last evening to see what it looked like. There was a game going and I sat into it. Fellow there who'd brought a gold dredger up river last year. The barge was part of the equipment for hauling this and that. Flood water last winter wrecked the dredger and the barge had been tied up at the bank ever since. This fellow was in the game and sort of reckless and wasn't going too well. He finally hit the bottom of his poke and offered to put the barge up as a stake. Bill and I had seen the barge when we went up to town and I asked Bill if he thought it was any good. Bill said it was, so we dealt the hand. The fellow's luck was still bad, and—well, there you are.'

Captain Bill said, a gleam in his eye, 'The idea was in my mind, soon as I first saw that barge. First thing this morning I had the boys drift it down and bring it alongside. Then we went ashore and cut a lot of pin oaks to build that railing. We can tow that barge and haul a flock of cattle on it and get the herd to San Francisco just that much quicker. What do you think, Jeff?'

'It sounds all right to me,' Jeff admitted. 'But the barge belongs to Harry and—'

Travers waved a hand. 'Didn't cost me a red—and I can't use it. Take it and welcome, for my food and transportation. For I'm making this trip down river with you. First time in more years than I like to remember that I ever got anywhere around something that was worthwhile, instead of cards and chips and men with the greed hunger shining far back in their eyes. It's going to do me a lot of good, just to be part of a deal like this. And that's all I want out of it—just to be a part.'

In the light of early dawn they began the loading. At first the cattle were stubborn and hard to handle, but after two or three had been driven up the gangplank the others began to follow and by mid morning the full three hundred head of the advance herd was aboard the boat and the barge. The cattle were edgy and nervous over these strange surroundings, but the bulwarks and rails were high and strong and the animals gradually quieted.

Jeff sent old Buck Yarnell back to join Stony Peters and the others with the main herd, but took the other two riders and their broncs aboard. Then the *Flame of Sunset* cast off and, with the loaded barge sliding along astern on a bridle tow, started the down stream run.

Captain Bill, his pipe stoked and going furiously, grinned at Jeff. 'Deep water bound, lad. I'd like to see the look on the faces of Colonel Nate Sharpe and Captain Noah Carlin when we go sliding by.'

'Just so we get by,' said Jeff.

What with the push of the current behind them, they made such good time during the half day run, they were over the most treacherous water by dusk. So Captain Bill ordered up plenty of hot coffee and got set for an all night run, too.

'I can take her in from here blindfolded, lad,' he told Jeff. 'Come tomorrow we'll be in water deep enough and wide enough for you or Harry to take the wheel while I catch up on a few winks of sleep.'

If Jeff had cause to wonder at the manner in which Captain Bill Ballinger had ferreted out safe waters during the daylight trip upstream, he had double cause to marvel at the grizzled riverman's uncanny judgment through the night with only the stars to give him light. So tricky were the massed shadows, so deceiving the faint, reflected glow from the water, that dozens of times Jeff found himself holding his breath and bracing himself in anticipation of crashing into the bank. But always what Jeff thought was bank turned out to be shadow and what he took to be shadow turned out to be bank, while Captain Bill's judgment of either never erred once, as he stood calmly, feet spread, pipe going, his big hands nursing the wheel.

With the push of the current to aid her, the *Flame of Sunset* urged steadily on and on, her tow swinging true and steady astern. Except for an occasional plaintive bellow, the cattle were quiet enough and one of the hands Jeff had brought along observed, 'Durned if the critters don't seem to be enjoyin' this here boat ride. Well, mebbe if I'd walked clear from Texas, like they have, I'd be willin' to settle for a ride, myself.'

'Maybe you got something there, Soapy,' chuckled Jeff. 'Even in the saddle, that trail was plenty long.'

Soapy spat overside. 'For takin' a herd through rustler country, this is sure the boss setup, Jeff. Was a crowd of wild ones set to jump us and put the critters to runnin', they're plumb out of luck. All they kin do is squat on the bank like a flock of hungry coyotes and beller at the stars, with us sliding by safe and sound under—'

Spang!

The rifle shot sounded clear and sharp from the east bank and there followed the tinkle of glass as the bullet crashed into the pilot house. It seemed to be a signal, for nearly a score of other shots rattled and snarled, winking in bright deadliness and sending a hail of lead crashing into the port side of the *Flame of Sunset.*

From the pilot house Captain Bill Ballinger's great voice roared his surprised anger. 'Get up here, Jeff!' he yelled. 'Get up here! Bring something for a barricade. They're aiming to get me or keep me from running a true wheel, so we'll pile up and wreck on the bank. Bring mattresses, or something for a barricade!'

★   ★   ★

Jeff gathered up mattress and blankets from his cabin, then climbed the ladder to the pilot house. He pushed his way in, a bullet fanning his cheek. 'Bill! Bill—you're all right?'

'Right enough! Get that stuff up here to port—my left! That's it. I shoulda guessed something of this sort and been ready for it. Stack it up!'

Even as Jeff worked he felt the shock of a

bullet smacking into the mattress, which muffled and stopped the slug. Harry Travers came in, carrying more bedding and stacked it up until, by crouching a little, Captain Bill was effectively bulwarked against any ordinary rifle fire on his left. No shots had come from the west bank and it was soon apparent that the attack was concentrated entirely on the east.

By this time two rifles were snarling a reply from the boat and Jeff knew that Soapy and Sling, his two riders, were at work. Jeff told Harry Travers, 'You stay here and hold this stuff up, Harry. I'm getting in on this!'

He dropped down the ladder, got his rifle out of his cabin, sought a vantage point and began shooting at the rifle flashes along the bank. It was tricky aiming, with the odds all against finding a billet for his searching lead. Yet either Sling or Soapy got a slug home, for a stricken yell sounded from the bank, and the hostile fire became momentarily ragged and uncertain.

Jeff muttered savagely, 'The dirty whelps! They wouldn't stand up to an open fight in daylight at all.'

It was apparent, from the way the fire from the bank kept up with the speeding *Flame of Sunset*, that the renegades were mounted and intended keeping up a running attack. It was also plain what their purpose was. Captain Bill had guessed it with the first shot. If they could keep the wheel from being properly manned and controlled, the *Flame of Sunset* would inevitably come to grief. This was particularly true of the stretch right ahead, for here the river made a sweeping turn to the east, then almost sharply straightened out to the south once more, and the drive of the current was bound to swing the boat in close to the east bank. Without calm and expert hands on the wheel, here would be the place where the crash would come.

The *Flame of Sunset* foamed into the bend and Jeff saw the east bank lift closer and closer above him, until but a few short yards separated it from the boat. But here the trees along the bank thinned out and the angle was such that Jeff could mark the rim of the bank against the stars. And onto this rim, looming in black silhouette, surged a group of riders.

It was the first time Jeff had had any definite target to shoot at. His rifle crashed. Then, because the range was so short, he dropped that weapon and went for his belt guns, emptying them into the blot of horses and men. Soapy and Sling did not miss this chance either. Between them and Jeff they brought down men and horses in wild tumult.

Here was something the renegades had not expected. They had anticipated little armed resistance and had gambled that the darkness and the shelter of the river bank would enable them to attack in complete safety. Now they had run into a deadly moment that had cost them dear. The survivors scattered wildly and by the time they recovered enough to renew the attack, the *Flame of Sunset* and her tow were safely through the tricky waters of the bend. Behind, the shooting died away and the river was once more still except for the panting of engine exhaust, the pound of paddle wheel and the lisp of sliding waters.

Jeff climbed to the pilot house and found Harry Travers tying a silk handkerchief about a bullet slash in Bill Ballinger's forearm. Captain Bill was profanely triumphant.

'They had a pretty scheme figured out there, if it had worked,' he growled. 'They made the mistake of showing their hand a little too quick. They should have waited until we swung in close to the bank at the bend, then they'd have had us dead to rights. As it is, well, let's see what Noah Carlin and Nate Sharpe can think up next. We're still a long way from San Francisco.'

Jeff said grimly, 'They've thought up a big plenty, already. I don't intend going through this sort of thing with every load of cattle we take down river. We get this load through, and I'm having a showdown with those two hombres.'

★   ★   ★

The rest of the night run was made without incident and by dawn Captain Bill estimated they were not over half a day above Sacramento. They were into deep, safe water and Captain Bill turned the wheel over to Harry Travers while he caught a few winks of sleep.

Jeff stood beside the quiet, imperturbable gambler, and found himself liking the man better all the time. He marked the gleam of deep pleasure and satisfaction in the gambler's eyes as he stood there at the wheel, holding the *Flame of Sunset* safely to the deep center of the channel. Travers, evidently guessing something of what was in Jeff's mind, said gravely, 'This is the sort of thing a man should do. Playing cards for a living is a dog's existence. I'm through with it. I'll work as a deck hand before I'll go back to the old life. Good-bye Harry Travers, gambler.'

A couple of hours of sleep was all Captain Bill needed and he was back at the wheel again when they hove in sight of Sacramento. They did not stop, but Jeff's glance reached past the crowded waterfront, toward the upper end of town, as though he would see past and through the shrouding groves of oak trees to the house of Colonel Nathaniel Sharpe. He thought of the type of man Sharpe was and of the kind of girl Sharpe's daughter was, and tried to reconcile the contrast, without success. Calm reason told him to put any thought of this girl from his mind, once and for all, because she was the daughter of a man who, with each passing day, was becoming a greater enemy. But when reason had finished presenting its case, emotion relived certain magic moments and Jeff knew that he would never again be free of the spell of Deborah Sharpe.

A mile below Sacramento a small rowboat pulled out from the bank, plainly intent on intercepting the *Flame of Sunset*. Captain Bill warned the small boat with a blast of his whistle, but the little craft came on, its single occupant, a bearded old river rat, glancing over his shoulder as he measured his approach. When but a few yards outside the course of the *Flame*, he spun the little boat around, drew something from a pocket and tossed it aboard. Then he waved and started back to the shore.

Soapy, Jeff's rider, retrieved the object. It was a sheet of paper, tightly wrapped about a small stone to give it weight. When Jeff freed the paper and smoothed it in his hands, he saw it was a written message, addressed to Captain Bill Ballinger. It said:

Bill:
  Beware of the Gold Camp. *It pulled out*

early this morning with a fine gang of cutthroats aboard. I always did say that at heart Noah Carlin was a first rate river pirate. Tell Jeff Kennett that he has a finer friend in the Nate Sharpe household than he knows.

Lizzie Jackson

Captain Bill Ballinger scowled as he read the message. A growl rumbled in his throat. 'Hard to convince, Noah Carlin. Good old Lizzie! There's one fine woman, Jeff—is Lizzie. And,' he added with a sly grin, 'I'd say there was another fine one, a young one, in the picture somewhere. So Noah Carlin pushed off in the *Gold Camp* early this morning, and with a gang of roughs aboard, eh? Well—well. That means that when that crowd who did that shooting at us up river failed to wreck us, they did some fast riding to hit Sacramento ahead of us and give the sad news to Carlin. And he figures on another try at us, somewhere between here and San Francisco. Well, I doubt Noah Carlin will make his try until somewhere below Rio Vista, and that suits me right down to the keel. I think I can interest Johnny Galway in this. I think I can.'

Jeff stared out at the brown waters ahead, and for mile after mile saw more and more country open on either side of the river. Here the great valley seemed steadily to widen until the rich plains spread endlessly on either hand while the far rims of distant mountains faded out until they were but faint smudges of hazy blue, distant and vague. They entered a delta country of vast size, with channels and sloughs opening and winding off from the main waterway, a land of black, peat-like earth, incredibly rich. Holding the wheel steady with his foot, Captain Bill stoked and lighted his stubby pipe, then waved a great hand to the east and south.

'There's a thousand miles of waterway out in there,' he said. 'And I don't know of any man who's sailed even a small part of it. I heard tell of men who've gone in there and never been heard of again. I can believe it. Someday, maybe, should things get too quiet along the river, I may try a look-see myself.'

'It's an empire, this country,' said Jeff soberly. 'And it's the land, the range that counts. That will last long after they've dug all the gold out of the gulches.'

With the coming of sunset the plains to the west rolled up into an expanse of low, rounded, grassy hills, and where the foot of these touched the river bank, rambling lines of low buildings marked another river town.

'Rio Vista,' Captain Bill said. 'And, by gravy, as I hoped, there's the *Antelope*, still tied up, waiting for that new boiler. Now we'll see if Johnny Galway isn't tired of just laying around, and would like a little fun for a change.'

Captain Bill maneuvered the *Flame of Sunset* gently in against the side of the steamboat tied up at a rude wharf. A stocky, broad, immensely powerful looking man in undershirt and greasy dungarees appeared on the *Antelope* and Captain Bill sent out a cheerful bellow.

'Come aboard, you bog trotting son of Satan, before I come over there after you!'

The stocky man hopped nimbly over the rail and climbed to the *Flame*'s pilot house, a broad grin on his face. He said, in a thick, rich brogue, 'Keep a civil tongue in your head, you bellowing bull, or I'll be after teachin' you some manners.'

Captain Bill and the newcomer struck hands and matched grins. 'Could I interest you in a little fracas, Johnny Galway?' Ballinger asked.

'Hum!' said Captain Johnny Galway. 'Sure and that depends. I admit time is growin' a bit weary on me hands, But I'll have none of your deviltry, Bill Ballinger, until I know more about it. What's your connivin' soul figuring on now?'

So Bill told him and Johnny Galway's blue eyes took on a gleam. ''Tis a fool I am for letting you lead me and my lads astray, but bein' a weak man and with little use for Noah Carlin and his ways, I admit to bein' interested.'

Captain Bill chuckled. 'Go get your lads, Johnny.'

So Johnny Galway went back aboard the *Antelope* and disappeared. But he soon returned, and following him were a round dozen men, who immediately scattered to mingle with the crew of the *Flame of Sunset*. Captain Bill brought the *Flame* around in another wide sweep and resumed steady progress down stream. He introduced Jeff Kennett to Johnny Galway and then swapped river news with Galway.

Now the river began a gradual sweep to the west and in thickening dusk the *Flame of Sunset* moved out into wide bay waters, her prow pointed straight into the last, lingering rose glow of the sunset sky. Here a quickening breeze met them and the water ridged with small, dancing white caps which sloshed and gurgled under the forefoot.

Johnny Galway tipped his snub nose and sniffed the air. 'We'll be in fog within an hour, Bill,' he said. 'That should help you.'

The stars came out and the air began to mist up until presently the stars faded and were gone. The air took on a wet, chill feel and the distant shore lines lost themselves in the thickening dark.

Jeff Kennett and his two riders, Soapy and Sling, had never been in such surroundings before. The two riders, gaunt and saddle leaned, sought out Jeff and Soapy inquired anxiously, 'How do we know where we're headin', Jeff? Sling and me don't savvy this kind of a trail. Suppose this oversize water bug sinks—then what?'

Jeff chuckled. 'I'm just as much a pilgrim at this sort of thing as you boys. I'm leaving it up to Captain Bill. He seems to know what he's doing.'

'Ruckus comin' up, ain't they?' asked Sling. 'We didn't stop up above and take that bunch of hefties aboard for nothin'.'

'Probably a ruckus,' Jeff nodded. 'I hope not, but if there is one, we'll meet it right on the nose.'

Abruptly faint lights appeared ahead in the mist and a whistle gave a hoarse, lonely challenge. Captain Bill answered in kind, and presently a big craft, full of lights and sending strains of music across the night, went sliding by, headed upstream.

'*River Queen*,' said Bill Ballinger succinctly. 'Biggest and fastest boat on the run. Caters to the fancy trade. Don't want any of her in mine. You got to dress for dinner and they catch you eating with your knife they throw you overboard.'

Soon all sight and sound of the *River Queen* was gone and the *Flame of Sunset* went her steady, lonely way. The mist was thickening. Then Johnny Galway said, 'Hah!

There she is, Bill. Port bow. There's the *Gold Camp*!'

CHAPTER EIGHT

At first Jeff could only pick up some pale lights, but then he saw the dark, looming bulk of the boat sliding along and coming gradually closer. 'Can't hope to outrun her,' said Captain Bill bluntly. 'But if that damned fog would only hurry up and get here, we'll make ourselves hard to find.'

Jeff wondered about that fog. To him it already seemed that the mist was thick enough to cut, but this apparently was not what Captain Bill was looking and hoping for. And then he found the difference. Ahead the night seemed incredibly black, and, as the *Flame of Sunset* thrust into it, she was instantly dripping wet. The air was surcharged with moisture, thick enough to taste.

This was fog, indeed. There was no sight or sound to signify that any other boat was within a thousand miles of the *Flame of Sunset*. To Jeff it seemed that there was nothing else in the world outside of himself, the small space of deck which supported his feet, and this ghostly, wet medium of fog. He fumbled his way about, found the pilot house beside him and heard Captain Bill and

Johnny Galway talking.

'Keep her bearing as she is, Bill,' advised Johnny Galway. 'Hold her that way for a couple of minutes then shut her down complete.'

Jeff waited, trying to hear something, trying to see something. A bell tinkled, deep in the engine room. The paddle wheels slowed and stopped and stillness lay over the *Flame of Sunset*, the only sound being the faint, faint lapping of the water under the forefoot. Then, back on the barge a steer bawled forlornly, and was answered by one on the cargo deck.

'Oh—oh!' said Johnny Galway. 'That's a foghorn we can't shut off. Playin' it quiet won't help us any. Might as well keep diggin' along and hope for the best. Maybe we can lose Carlin. If we can't, then he can have his little fight.'

So the bell tinkled again, the wheels took up their measured thrashing and the *Flame* bored ahead. But soon the thumping of another paddle wheel came out of the fog and with it, dim and menacing and ghostly, the faint radiance of lights, like misty yellow eyes. Soon the towering superstructure of the *Gold Camp* was almost on top of them.

Captain Bill swung the wheel again and for a few moments they lost the menace of their pursuer. Johnny Galway said, 'Can't keep on bearing away, Bill. Else we'll have mud under our keel, first thing we know. Tide's on the ebb, and if we hit the mud we stay there until the next flood.'

'I know it,' growled Captain Bill. 'Better go get the boys organized, Johnny. Next time the *Gold Camp* shows, I'm going to lay the *Flame* alongside and Noah Carlin can have what he's askin' for. He's going to be almighty surprised to find we got better than twice as many fighting men aboard as he figured on.'

Johnny Galway hurried off and Jeff asked, 'What could he hope to profit, Bill? Carlin, I mean?'

'Three hundred head of cattle,' said Bill dryly. 'Plus bustin' up us and the *Flame*, so we'd be all through haulin' any of the rest of the herd. Block you off from market and make you come to his terms. There's a big stake in your two thousand head of cattle, lad—a big stake, as you'll find when you see the prices you'll be offered at San Francisco—providing we ever get there. Men have robbed and killed for less—a lot less. And Noah Carlin, besides hatin' you and me, bitter, is just what Lizzie Jackson said he was—a pirate at heart. We're fightin' for plenty, so don't waste your punches.'

The wet, blank, blind minutes ticked by and Jeff was beginning to hope that they had shaken pursuit, when Captain Bill swore softly. 'Here he comes again. He's like a shark following a blood trail.'

Once more Jeff saw those pale, malevolent, yellow light eyes peering through the fog, then the ghostly shadow of the *Gold Camp*'s superstructure. She came sliding in at a long angle and it was a case of the *Flame* either altering course again, or accepting inevitable contact. Captain Bill Ballinger gave not an inch, except to swing the *Flame* just enough to keep the contact from being too heavy.

Closer, closer towered the *Gold Camp*. There was a scraping jar and the splintering of some woodwork. And then they came swarming, the men of Noah Carlin's crew. Over the grinding, jostling rails they poured, intent on winning quick mastery of the *Flame* with her smaller crew. Several of them charged for the pilot house and Jeff met this group head on. He landed one clean, solid blow, dropping his man. Then the weight of numbers swept him up and drove him back and left him fighting for his very life.

He must inevitably have been crushed and beaten down, but from the pilot house came a roaring challenge and Captain Bill Ballinger struck the fighting group like a runaway hurricane. The pressure on Jeff immediately slackened and enabled him to win back a little ground.

Another shout echoed, further aft on the *Flame*. It was the voice of Captain Johnny

Galway of the *Antelope*, and it was a war cry full of taunting mockery. It was answered by a yell of dismay and warning from one of the *Gold Camp* gang, who now found themselves in a much tougher fight than they had bargained for.

Their anticipated easy conquest not being realized, the rough gang from the *Gold Camp* started a grimmer, more deadly business. Clubs began to swish through the air. Jeff ducked under one of these, came to grips with the wielder and rushed him across the deck, backing the fellow up against the rail. There he stayed close in, beating his man in the face until the fellow toppled backward and, with a shriek of terror, dropped into that black, grinding cavern between the two boats.

Jeff swung around, spat out a mouthful of blood and charged back into the fight. Captain Bill, battered and bleeding, but still on his feet, had torn a pick handle from one of the attackers with such violence that the fellow was shambling around, mumbling and groaning over a dislocated arm. And now Captain Bill was swinging the pick handle around and around in such wild, berserk violence that the circle of attackers began to break up and scatter. Jeff slugged one of them under the ear, tore the fellow's club from him as he fell, and waded in, swinging right and left. He felt a man's arm crack cleanly under one lashing blow and stabbed the end of the club full into a cursing, snarling face which loomed palely before him. The face disappeared.

A triumphant cry sounded from Johnny Galway, showing that the fight was going well back aft. Jeff and Captain Bill felt a new surge of strength and confidence and they continued to wade in, clubs swinging wickedly. Came another yell, thick and hoarse with range and disappointment.

'*Gold Camp* men! Back to your own boat—back to your own boat!'

Captain Bill roared exultantly. 'They're licked—licked. Give 'em hell, Jeff! Give 'em hell!'

Jeff needed no added incentive. He tore into the faltering enemy, driving them back and back. One of them threw a club and it came in low, nearly cutting Jeff's feet from under him. Sharp agony followed the blow and Jeff floundered a moment before getting his footing solidly under him again. Then he leaped on the club thrower. They crashed into the rail and one grinding uneasily against it, and landed on the deck of the *Gold Camp*, where they fought on in a panting, cursing tangle.

There were no rules to this game. Jeff got his man by locking his fingers about the burly, unshaven throat and pounding the fellow's head on the deck of the *Gold Camp* until he went limp. Then, as he struggled to his feet a wave of charging men hit him, knocking him down again, scrambling over him. *Gold Camp* men, fleeing from the *Flame of Sunset*, were swarming back to the security of their own boat.

Somewhere close by a voice was shouting, 'Sheer off—sheer off!'

The deck trembled under Jeff as the *Gold Camp*'s engines began to strain and her paddle wheel lashed and pounded the black waters. Realization of his peril struck him like a dousing of icy water. The *Gold Camp* was pulling away from the *Flame of Sunset*, and he was on the *Gold Camp*.

Jeff Kennett fought bitterly but futilely. By the time his hammering fists broke a pathway to the rail, he saw despairingly that already there was a ten foot gap of black emptiness between the two boats and the gap was steadily widening. To have tried to leap it would have been suicidal.

The instinct to yell, to call to the *Flame*, sent words into his panting, raw throat, but he held back the words, knowing their uselessness. Behind him a voice snarled, 'Right there, against the rail. Off the *Flame of Sunset*—!'

Jeff turned and took a sledge hammer blow in the face. It numbed him, blinded him, sent his senses wavering. He staggered forward a step or two, hands pawing instinctively but weakly. Another of those cruel blows crashed home and it seemed to Jeff Kennett as though a sudden high wind had picked him up and was whirling him away into deep, black depths. Vaguely he felt the impact of the deck as he fell. Then his senses left him.

* * *

When Jeff came to he found himself lying on a bunk, staring up at the white painted confines of a cabin. He blinked painfully, rolled his head and groaned a trifle at the swift, stabbing pain this movement brought. There was a stir and then a rawboned figure stood over him. It was Captain Noah Carlin.

'So you're not dead after all, eh?' growled Carlin. 'I was a little afraid I'd hit you too solidly. Your head is not only thick, but hard, it seems. Not feeling quite so wild and woolly and cocksure as usual, eh? Maybe you wish you had made a deal with me in the first place?'

Jeff ran his tongue across his battered lips and said nothing. His mind was clearing rapidly and he was quite content to lie there, resting his bruised and aching head and body. Noah Carlin had something in mind and the smart thing to do was wait until he got ready to show his hand. As everything began coming back to him, Jeff knew one satisfaction. Carlin had neither the *Flame of Sunset*, nor the cattle.

Noah Carlin took a short turn up and down the little cabin. The *Gold Camp* was beating a steady way along. Jeff could feel the vibration of the engines, the pound of the paddle wheel. Abruptly Carlin stopped his pacing, stood over Jeff. 'How,' he demanded, 'did Galway and his gang happen to be on the *Flame of Sunset?*'

Jeff's grin was painful and lopsided. 'That surprised you, eh? Good man, Johnny Galway.'

'That's not answering my question. Don't get proud, Kennett. I'd just as soon knock you on the head and throw you overboard as not.'

Jeff stared up at the man and realized that this was true enough. There was a cold blooded look about Noah Carlin. Jeff said, 'After that attack higher up river, it seemed reasonable enough to expect you to make another try, before we got the cattle safe to San Francisco. So, we took on a few more hands, just in case.'

Carlin studied him with cold and measuring eyes. 'I think you are lying. I think somebody tipped you off. I aim to find out about that. And if somebody did—!' Jeff saw Carlin clench his fists and grind his jaw.

Jeff shrugged. 'Captain Bill Ballinger is pretty long headed.'

Rage and hate lay naked and ugly in Carlin's eyes. 'The hand isn't played out yet, not by a whole lot,' he blurted, 'as both you and Ballinger are due to find out. And Galway will wish he'd minded his own business, too.' With this, Carlin stamped out, slamming and locking the cabin door behind him.

Jeff lay quiet for a time, thinking. That load of cattle? Bill Ballinger could be depended upon to take it on to San Francisco and make the best deal possible. In the meantime, Jeff wondered if Bill would figure out what had happened to him, and decided that he probably would. Bill had been fighting right alongside of him when he rushed that rough to the rail and then followed him over on to the *Gold Camp*. For the time, Jeff concluded, there was nothing he could do except take it easy and wait for the future. With this sensible conclusion he closed his aching eyes, relaxed and fell asleep.

★ ★ ★

He awoke to a hand on his shoulder, shaking him roughly. It was Noah Carlin. The ship's lights were out and Carlin was just a bulky, menacing shadow against the first pale gray light of dawn, stealing through the cabin windows.

'Get moving!' growled Carlin, and as Jeff stumbled sleepily to his feet the muzzle of a gun was jammed against him. 'One of your own,' Carlin warned him. 'And if you try and raise a row or pull any other fancy business, I'll shoot your spine in half. Outside!'

The *Gold Camp* was now berthed along the Sacramento river front. At the muzzle of that jabbing gun, Noah Carlin herded Jeff Kennett across the gangplank and up town by a circuitous route, taking no chances of their being observed. Their destination, as Jeff had already guessed, was the Colonel Sharpe home, set back in its grove of oaks.

They went to a side door and Noah Carlin produced a key to give them entrance. They went along a short, dark hall and into an equally dark room. With his free hand Carlin lighted a lamp, which showed the small limits of the room. It contained only a bed and a chair and a small, flat-topped bureau. The single window was heavily shuttered on the outside.

'You'll have time to do a little thinking, Kennett,' Carlin said. 'Better start thinking sensible and realize I'm playing this game for keeps. If you figure you can break out, figure again. The shutters outside that window are plenty stout and by the time you battered them off, I'd be waiting for you with this.' Carlin waved the gun. Then he backed out, closing the door, and the lock clicked.

Jeff did think, and it got him nowhere in particular. It was the sort of game where a man just had to sit back and wait for the opposition to show its hand. He knew that by this time daylight must be strong outside, but no hint of it showed through that heavily shuttered window. Physically, aside from the soreness of his bruises, Jeff felt about normal and it came to him abruptly that he was ravenously hungry.

The hours drifted by. Very faintly Jeff heard sounds of stirring life about the house. He wondered about Deborah Sharpe. A quick thrill ran through him with the realization that she was probably not many yards from him at this very moment. Then steps sounded in the hall and a key was in the lock. The door opened slowly and Jeff grinned wryly at the ready muzzle of the gun which preceded Noah Carlin in to the room. Behind him came Colonel Nate Sharpe.

'I'm still here,' drawled Jeff mockingly. 'And hungry—plenty. Fine brand of hospitality, this! If you're figuring on another jawing match, you might as well understand that I'm not even listening until I have something to eat.'

Noah Carlin scowled, then turned to his partner. 'Go bring him some breakfast,' he growled, in a tone such as he might have used on a servant. Colonel Sharpe flushed, but went back out without arguing. And this told Jeff Kennett something more. For while Noah Carlin and Colonel Nate Sharpe might pose as partners, it was Carlin who gave orders, and Sharpe who obeyed.

Carlin said abruptly, 'Just how did they get word to the *Flame of Sunset* that I would be waiting in the *Gold Camp* for you, down river?'

It was a question Noah Carlin had asked before, but he repeated it now in a calculated effort to surprise Jeff into some sort of startled giveaway. He nearly succeeded, but Jeff caught himself just in time. 'Persistent cuss, aren't you?' Jeff drawled. 'Asked that one before. I told you Captain Bill Ballinger is long headed.'

'Not that long headed,' snarled Carlin. 'He knew that the *Antelope* was tied up at Rio Vista for repairs, same as every other skipper along the river. But he wouldn't have gone to the trouble and expense of picking up Galway and his crew just on a gamble that I was waiting for him. He must have known it. And he couldn't have known it, unless somebody told him.'

Jeff shrugged. 'That's your idea. Play with it all you want.'

'There's an answer, and I'll find it,' vowed Carlin. 'And somebody will pay!'

Colonel Sharpe came in, carrying a tray loaded with food. He seemed jittery, and nearly spilled the jug of coffee as he set it down on the bureau. Jeff pulled up the chair and ate with honest hunger. When he finished, he built a smoke and squared around to face Carlin and Sharpe.

'I don't imagine you just came in to watch me eat,' he drawled. 'Maybe I'm guessing, but I figure you got another big hearted offer to make. I'm just telling you ahead of time that it won't do you a lick of good.'

Carlin cursed again. 'We'll see,' he growled. 'This time we're spreading all the cards on the table, face up. You happen to own a herd of cattle, Kennett, that is worth an awful lot of money. Well, I intend to take over that herd. You can make it easy for me and easy for yourself. Or you can make it a little more difficult for me, and damn hard for yourself. Just how hard, you'll find out later on, in case you turn out to be stubborn. I might tell you that when I sit into a game of big stakes, I play to win—and I do win.'

Jeff inhaled and sent a thin blue line of smoke from his pursed lips. 'Seems to me we went over that all before, right in this same house. Well, the answer I gave you then is the same answer I give you now.'

Noah Carlin's lips pulled into a thin, bitter line. 'And the answer I gave you then I'll enlarge on a little, now,' he gritted. 'With one difference. Instead of you holding the gun, I do. So here it is, Kennett—cold.

You'll write me out a bill of sale for that herd or you'll be turned over to the custody of Marshal Shag Taggart, on the charge of murder. Oh no, we haven't forgotten that man whose skull you crushed with a gun barrel. Not a bit of it. The man had a lot of friends, Kennett, who haven't forgotten it, either. There is nothing they would like better than to put a lynch rope around the neck of the man who killed him. So the chances are strong that, while Marshal Taggart is conducting you to the lockup, these men will take you away from him and use that lynch rope. In fact, I'd be willing to bet money that that is exactly what they will do. Be a good thing for Sacramento, a lynching for murder. Quite a salutary lesson, you might say.'

There was something in Carlin's tone like the purr of a feline playing with its quarry before killing it. Jeff Kennett looked at him, then at Colonel Nate Sharpe. The latter was pale, with a more obvious shiftiness about him than he had ever shown before.

'I ran into some pretty tough customers, coming across the plains with my herd,' Jeff said contemptuously. 'But the worst of them were gentlemen alongside as slimy a pair as you two. Now let me tell you something, once and for all. Every cent I have in the world is invested in that herd of cattle. But there is more than that invested. There's two years of driving, on one trail, and the companionship of men better than you have ever known. Some of those men lie buried back along that trail. Those who lived, brought the herd through. They swam wild rivers, they fought wild tribes, but they brought the cattle through. Do you think I'd sell out those men by knuckling under to a pair of crooks? Even if I didn't own a hair on one of those cow-critters, I wouldn't let those boys down. Now you got it—you got my answer. And it will never change, regardless.'

Noah Carlin pulled a crooked smirk. 'Very touching little tale—very. We'll see what you have to say when that lynch rope is around your neck.'

Jeff's laugh held a harsh, barking note. 'Listen, Carlin. There were tough men out there along the trail who tried to stop me—tougher than you ever thought of being. Well, I'm here. And another little point for you to remember. The boys waiting up river with that herd are waiting for me. If I don't show up by the time I'm expected to, they'll come looking. Tough, those boys can be, when they have to. They'll have a gun on each hip and one across their saddles. Should the idea hit them, they'll take this town apart like no town was ever taken apart before. And you and Sharpe—well, I wouldn't want to be in your boots. Lynching will be easy alongside of what they'll do to you.'

Carlin smirked again. 'I don't scare easy, myself, Kennett. Your last word, eh?'

'I said so, didn't I?'

Noah Carlin backed to the door, still holding that ready gun. 'We'll see what you have to say when you hear the voice of the mob. Ever hear the voice of a mob, Kennett? Sound you'll never forget. And when you hear the voice of this one, you'll know who they're coming for. All right, Nate—bring out those dishes.'

Colonel Nathaniel Sharpe was pale and sweating. 'There may be—some other way. Perhaps—if we talked—'

'We've talked enough,' cut in Noah Carlin savagely. 'This bright fellow thinks I'm bluffing. He'll know better shortly. Bring that stuff along—and don't forget the knife and fork!'

CHAPTER NINE

Pacing slowly up and down the narrow confines of this prison room, Jeff Kennett measured the setup. Carlin was tenacious, once he set himself to a purpose. Three times had he tried to wreck Jeff's plan for transporting cattle. Three times he had failed, and he was a man who could not brook failure. Besides, he hated Jeff blackly and bitterly, just as he hated Captain Bill Ballinger and as he no doubt in the future would hate Johnny Galway. Maybe that threat of the mob was very real. Maybe he would turn Jeff over to that mob.

The thought sent a little quiver up Jeff's spine. He went to the door, tried it, put the power and weight of his shoulder to it. It was massive, that door, with the weight and fibre of oak. No chance here.

He went to the window, slid the sash up, and tried the shutters. They were strong and solid and evidently barred on the outside. Given time, however, he could batter a way through there. He went back and picked up the chair. It was heavy enough. But not now, he decided. The first blow would spread an alarm and Carlin would be right back in there with a gun. The thing to do right now was think—think—!

He turned a dozen schemes over in his mind. None was sound. He tried to think of more, while the minutes ran away and a good hour passed. Then, faint but unmistakable, he heard beyond those barred shutters the first concerted roar and rumble of massed voices. He moved over to the window and stood there, ears straining. He heard it again, a little louder. The voice of a mob—!

So Carlin hadn't been bluffing, and it came in a flash to Jeff that once Carlin got a mob started, he couldn't stop it. He wouldn't dare, for then the mob, realizing it had been tricked and used to suit Carlin's own purpose, would turn on him. No, this was it!

Jeff slammed a clenched fist against the shutters. They rattled slightly, but gave not an inch. He went back to the chair, caught it, swung it high. But before the first crashing blow could fall, he stopped and turned. For the lock in the door had clicked.

It was in Jeff's mind to hurl the chair at whoever entered and take any chance that offered after that. Instead he stopped, dead still. It was Deborah Sharpe who stood in the doorway, and behind her was Aunt Amanda, her face set with a strange, grim purpose. The girl's eyes were dilated with fear. And fear was in her voice as she said, 'Quickly, Jeff—come! Can't you hear it? The mob? Oh, Jeff—hurry!'

Jeff lowered the chair, moved over. He looked at her as though unable to believe his senses. It was Aunt Amanda who said grimly, 'I know what you are thinking, young man—that this is a house of insanity. Well, I call it plain, idiotic foolishness and I have had enough of it. Noah Carlin may be able to wind Nate Sharpe around his little finger and lead him into all kinds of contemptible business, but he can't do as well with Debbie and me. You're getting out of here, young man—and you're taking Debbie with you. Hurry, now! Don't stand there gaping at me like a great booby. I'm quite sane and know exactly what I'm doing. Here, you may need this!'

Into Jeff's hand she pressed a beautifully engraved and silver-mounted six-shooter. Jeff was still dumbfounded.

'Come, come!' urged Aunt Amanda. 'You've no time to waste. Go out the back way, Debbie, and circle well back through the oaks. Lizzie Jackson is waiting for you and will see to it that you are well hidden.'

Jeff stuttered, 'But you, ma'am? If you stay here, Carlin may—'

Aunt Amanda waved a scornful hand. 'Noah Carlin may be able to bully my brother, but he'll not dare lay a finger on me. Now get along quickly—you two!'

She led them swiftly to the back door of the house and a second later they were scurrying away through the oaks. Jeff said, 'I don't like this. I don't like running away and leaving your aunt there to face Carlin alone. He'll frighten her to death.'

'No,' declared Debbie, 'he won't. Aunt Amanda may have fainted that—that day of the stage holdup—but when she gets her dander up, she can surprise you. And it is up, this time. Noah Carlin won't dare touch her.'

'Your father,' argued Jeff. 'How about your father?'

'We—we surprised him and locked him in his study. Carlin can't blame him. Please hurry, Jeff. There is nothing you can do.'

Off to their right they could hear the hoarse growl of the mob as it advanced up from town toward the Sharpe mansion. But as they swung wider and wider on their circle of escape, they left the sound behind. Soon they were beyond all limits of the town and cutting for the river front. This they found comparatively deserted, as all the able-bodied men had been caught up and sucked along by the excitement and morbid purpose of the mob. Finally, breathless and whimpering a little, Debbie Sharpe led Jeff Kennett into the back door of Lizzie Jackson's hotel.

'I was beginning to worry,' Lizzie scolded gently. 'I was afraid the mob had seen you and headed you off. Debbie, child, you run along to my room. Young man—this way.'

Before Jeff could say a word to Debbie, the girl was gone. He followed Lizzie to a small corner room, dusky behind down-pulled shades.

'This was Anse Jackson's room,' she said simply. 'Since his death, no one has ever been in it but me. Now you may use it while we wait for the *Flame of Sunset* to come back up the river.'

Jeff said doubtfully, 'This is kind of you, Mrs. Jackson. And it is fine of Debbie and her aunt to do all they have for me. But I can't hide behind the skirts of good women. I've got to get out and fight my own battle. I—'

'Nonsense!' broke in Lizzie Jackson briskly. 'What could you do, lone handed? There must be at least two hundred fool men in that mob. Most of those drunken idiots don't even know the why or how of things. They are just like sheep, following a leader—in this case, Shag Taggart, who is monkey-on-a-stick for Noah Carlin. Well, it has taken Debbie and Amanda Sharpe and Lizzie Jackson to fool them. Now make yourself at home in this room and leave matters up to us. We women know what we are doing.'

Back at the Sharpe home the mob was now massed before the mansion, milling about, growling its blind blood lust. Out in front was Shag Taggart, while off to one side stood Noah Carlin, apparently just a spectator, but watching with a cold eyed, malignant triumph.

Shag Taggart pounded on the door, but backed up rather hurriedly when Aunt Amanda Sharpe opened it and stepped out, a shotgun in her hands and a look of scorn on her face. At sight of her the mob stared in amazement. The growl quieted and Aunt Amanda's voice carried clearly and cuttingly.

'What is the meaning of this? What are you drunken fools up to, bawling and howling around, disturbing the peace of good citizens? Answer me! What is the meaning of this?' Aunt Amanda directed her blazing eyes and the muzzle of the shotgun directly at Shag Taggart. 'You seem to be leading these fools,' she flared. 'Suppose you talk for them. Or has the cat got your tongue?'

Shag Taggart gulped. 'There's a murderer in this house,' he blurted finally. 'We've come to get him.'

'You daft idiot!' scoffed Aunt Amanda. 'There is no such thing in this house. And even if there was, I'd have no such ruffian as you crossing my threshold. Be off, the whole drunken mess of you, before I shoot!'

Here was something Shag Taggart definitely had not expected. Had Aunt Amanda been a man, he would have known what to do. But it was one thing to lay rough hands on a man and shoulder him out of the way, while it was something entirely different to attempt the same tactics with a gray-haired woman, especially one with such a determined look in her eye and with a shotgun in her hands.

Taggart backed up another step and threw an anxious glance where Noah Carlin had been. But Carlin, his face dark as a thundercloud, had disappeared, circling the house, heading for the back door. Unable to think of anything better to do, Shag Taggart began, almost pleadingly, 'Listen, ma'am. We don't aim—'

'You don't aim at anything, Shag Taggart,' cut in Amanda Sharpe crisply. 'You're getting out of here, now!' She turned to face the mob. 'Go on back to your liquor pots, the whole filthy mess of you. The idea! Coming bawling and yelling around here, trying to frighten a gray-haired woman. What kind of men are you? For shame!'

Aunt Amanda was playing her cards skilfully. Under her words and scorn the mob grew uneasy. 'What's the big idea, Taggart?' a voice yelled. 'You told us there was a murderer. If that murderer is here, trot him out and we'll string him up, high and quick. But we didn't come to bully a woman.'

Shag Taggart didn't know what to do or know what to say. Meanwhile, the blind, unreasoning fever of the mob was cooling with stark rapidity. And now a ragged, mud-stained miner, obviously the worse for drink, stepped out a stride or two toward Aunt Amanda, took off his battered hat and bowed low, with a ridiculous alcoholic gravity.

'Lady,' he mumbled thickly, 'we beg—

your pardon. We are gentlemen—good men. We do not frighten women. We have been misled. You will—hic—excuse us.'

He bowed again and almost fell on his face. Then he straightened up with vastly overdone dignity, clapped his hat on his head, turned and moved away, weaving as he went.

This was all that was needed. Somebody laughed and the malignant spirit of the mob was gone entirely. Its members began to straggle away, several of them jeering at Taggart. Shag himself, thoroughly outwitted, followed helplessly.

Aunt Amanda, triumphant but with shaking knees, stepped back into the house, shut the door and leaned against it, closing her eyes momentarily. When she opened them, it was to find herself facing Noah Carlin, his face convulsed with fury.

'Where is he?' snarled Carlin. 'Quick! What have you done with Kennett? And where is that snivelling, spineless brother of yours? I've been double-crossed enough in this house. I'm going to—'

Aunt Amanda had straightened again to her full dignity. 'You're going to get out of this house, once and for all, Noah Carlin—and you'll never enter it again. You have made a fool of my brother, but you'll never make a fool of me. I am the mistress of this household and I tell you to get gone and stay gone.'

Noah Carlin tried to match the blazing spirit in Amanda Sharpe's eyes. 'Nate Sharpe can't back out on me now,' he blurted. 'Before I'm done—'

'You'd better go,' cut in Amanda Sharpe. 'I'm not going to tell you again.' And as she spoke she raised her shotgun to her shoulder.

There was nothing Noah Carlin could do but obey. Black and consuming as was his rage, he knew that here was checkmate, at least for the moment. This woman would shoot, if she had to—and with a shotgun, at this range, she would not miss. He went out, slamming the door behind him so savagely the whole house shook.

Aunt Amanda sidled over to a handy chair, dropped into it and began to weep a little. But the tears were merely the result of a nervous letdown. So soon she brushed them aside and even mustered up the glimmerings of a grim smile.

'Shades of your august ancestors, Amanda Sharpe!' she murmured. 'What would your circle of Boston friends have thought if they could have seen you waving this shotgun at that mob of drunken fools? What would they have thought? And who cares? For the first time in your life you have really begun to live. Truly this is a golden, magic country. And now to let Nate Sharpe out of his study and give him a dressing down that will bruise his pride terribly, but do his immortal soul a world of good!'

CHAPTER TEN

It was late in the afternoon of the second day following when the *Flame of Sunset* came thrashing back up river to Sacramento, towing the empty barge. Her cargo deck was empty and scrubbed clean. Captain Bill Ballinger, grim and anxious-looking, eased the *Flame* into a berthing and was the first man across the gangplank; but crowding close behind him were Soapy and Sling. There was a hard, bitter look about the eyes of these two, and Soapy said harshly, 'We're staying with you, Bill, until you put the price of that load of cattle in a safe place. Then we're goin' to find this Carlin hombre and fill him full of holes. We're evenin' up for Jeff Kennett if it's the last thing we ever do.'

'Take it a little slow, boys,' cautioned Captain Bill. 'I still think Jeff is all right. I'm telling you again, I saw him go over the rail on to the *Gold Camp*'s deck. He didn't go into the water. Carlin has got him prisoner somewhere. You go to shooting things up regardless, and you won't help matters a bit. Wait until we ask a few questions. We'll get a line on Jeff. You'll see.'

An old river rat, the same who had tossed the message onto the *Flame*, came sidling up. 'Lizzie Jackson wants to see you, Bill—right away. Real important.'

Captain Bill nodded and started for the Jackson House, Soapy and Sling following grimly along. Tucked up under one arm, Bill Ballinger carried a squat, heavy canvas sack. At her usual place in the hotel, Lizzie sat knitting calmly. She looked up and said, 'High time you were showing, Bill Ballinger. What kept you down river so long?'

'Well,' growled Bill, 'the *Flame of Sunset* never was a fast packet, and now, towing that barge—. Besides, there were other things to do, such as landing the cattle, selling them and getting payment.' He patted the canvas sack. 'But we got bigger worries than that. Carlin has Jeff Kennett prisoner on the *Gold Camp*, and—'

'Did have him, you mean,' corrected Lizzie Jackson. 'If you hadn't berthed pretty quick I don't know how I could have kept that young man under cover much longer. He's been like a caged panther. Come along and take him off my hands.' She led the way to the little room, drew a key from the pocket of her apron and unlocked the door. 'All right, my wild eagle,' she called, as she swung the door wide. 'The cage is open. You can fly, now.'

Jeff Kennett fell on Captain Bill and the

two faithful punchers like an avalanche. 'Bill—Soapy—Sling!—Do you look good to me! Tell me everything. How about the cattle? How about—?'

'Easy, lad—easy,' growled the captain. 'The main thing is—you're all right. Here's your cattle.' And he shoved the canvas sack into Jeff's hands, grinning. 'Nine thousand dollars worth, in gold.'

Jeff lifted the heavy sack and gulped. 'Nine thou—! Why—why that's thirty dollars a head.'

'Exactly,' nodded Captain Bill. 'Thirty a head, herd run, as Soapy here would say. And an offer for all the rest at the same price.'

Jeff looked dumbfounded. 'I paid eight dollars a head for them in Texas. I figured if I could double my money I could pay all expenses and still have a pretty good stake left. But thirty a head—why, that's sixty thousand for the lot. No wonder Noah Carlin seems ready to commit murder or anything else to get his hands on that herd!'

'This Carlin hombre,' growled Soapy. 'Where at do you think me and Sling can corner him, Jeff? We got a little unfinished business with that juniper.'

'Which makes three of us,' said Jeff, suddenly grim. 'I've been skulking long enough to keep out of his hands. Now I go looking for him.' He turned to Lizzie

Jackson, held out the canvas sack. 'You keep it for me, ma'am. You're one of the three best women in this world. Take what I owe you for board and room out of it and then chuck it under your bed. Take plenty. I can't be bothered lugging it around with me. It'll be safer in your hands.'

Lizzie Jackson nodded. 'I'll take care of it for you. I'm sorry I had to lock that door. But it was the only way I could keep you from going out and getting yourself killed.'

'Where—where's Debbie?' Jeff asked. 'I haven't had a chance to thank her for getting me away from that mob.'

'She's back home now—and quite safe,' said Lizzie Jackson. 'Amanda Sharpe has taken over in that household. She has denied Noah Carlin all entrance to the house and she has jerked that brother of hers into line in no uncertain fashion. Amanda Sharpe, in case you hadn't realized it, is quite a woman. You will also find that if all partnership between Colonel Nate Sharpe and Captain Noah Carlin has not already been dissolved, it very shortly will be. That's something else Amanda Sharpe is taking care of.'

Captain Bill Ballinger cut in. 'Mob? What's all this talk about a mob? Let's get over on the boat and set everything straight. Lizzie, you're a blessed angel for keeping the lad safe for us.'

Lizzie Jackson sniffed, but smiled. 'You

men—! Someone has to keep you straightened out. Be off with you, and see that you get in no further trouble.'

They went back to the *Flame* and gathered eagerly around while Jeff told of all that had happened to him since the *Gold Camp* pulled away in the fog. Harry Travers was there with the rest to listen in, and there was no mistaking his delight at seeing Jeff safe and sound. Travers had completely discarded the habiliments of his old trade and now wore the rough and ready clothes of a confirmed riverman. Exposure was beginning to drive the pallor from his face. Jeff found himself liking this quiet-voiced ex-gambler better all the time.

When Jeff finished his story, Soapy and Sling hitched up their gunbelts. 'I say again, let's go lookin' for this Carlin hombre,' growled Soapy. 'The sooner that feller is strung on a slug, the quicker and easier we can get on with our job of movin' cattle.'

'I doubt he's in town,' said Captain Bill. 'The *Gold Camp* isn't around, and wherever it is, that's where Noah Carlin will be. One thing is certain, though. There is more deviltry brewing.'

'When can we start up river for another load of cattle, Bill?'

'Soon as we fuel up and get some eating supplies aboard. Feeding Johnny Galway and his boys sort of cleaned us out. I think an early start tomorrow morning should be about right.'

'Fair enough,' Jeff nodded. 'That'll give me a chance to make a couple of calls I got in mind.'

'Don't you go wandering around this town too free and easy,' warned Bill Ballinger in quick alarm. 'No telling what you might run into. To some folks you're a marked man.'

'He ain't going alone,' said Soapy significantly. 'Sling and me are goin' to ride herd on him.'

Jeff grinned. 'Let's go, boys.'

★ ★ ★

As Jeff and his two riders left the *Flame*, Harry Travers dropped in with them. 'Where'd I be most liable to locate this Shag Taggart, Harry?' Jeff asked him.

'He hangs around the Eagle a lot,' said Travers.

'We'll drop in there,' nodded Jeff.

But they saw no sign of Taggart at the Eagle. Travers said, 'I got a few friends in here. I'll stick around and chin with them a while.'

Jeff and Soapy and Sling went on, dropping into this saloon and that. Jeff said, 'I never hid out from any man or bunch of men before in my life, but I guess Lizzie Jackson was right in insisting I stay cooped up in that room until the *Flame* came back up river. Maybe I would have run into more than I could handle had I gone it alone. But that sort of thing goes against a man's grain and I want no more of it.'

Soapy nodded. 'What this town needs is a little example in manners, and me and Sling aim to show it one, if somebody will just give us a chance.'

But Soapy and Sling had no chance to demonstrate. Nowhere could they find the slightest show of hostility, though they looked for it with anxious, eager eyes, ready at the drop of a hat to show the world they were not men to be trifled with. The rough river crowd had gone to ground, apparently, and the flood of miners, coming and going, had interest in nothing but the thing which glowed so feverishly in their eyes at all times—gold, and the search for it.

They ended up at the stage station, when Jeff drew Tom Hankins aside. 'Something I want to know, Hankins,' he said. 'You been in these parts quite a while, haven't you?'

'One of the old timers,' nodded Hankins. 'Came in with John Sutter in '39. Helped build his fort. Why?'

'That plains country along the river—is that all free land?'

Hankins pulled his under lip with thumb and forefinger. 'Hum! What you got in mind?'

'A ranch. Cattle and grain.'

Hankins nodded slowly. 'Smart man. That is the wealth in this country that will last, the land itself. Well, it's this way, Kennett. Most of the land is supposed to be under some sort of grant held by different Spanish dons. But their boundaries are loose and the titles even more so. They don't actually use a small fraction of it. A land rush is going to follow this gold rush and the claims of the dons won't stand up for a minute. I'd say the smart thing for you to do is pick the spot you like and get your ranch started. Then, when the showdown comes, what with improvements you put in and evidence of actually using the land in your favor, you'll not have too much trouble in making your claim stick.'

'I don't intend to take anything that doesn't belong to me,' said Jeff. 'I'll be willing to pay for what I want.'

'Then you are doubly armed,' said Hankins. 'Pick your layout and let it be known you'll pay to the man who can establish ownership beyond all doubt, and you won't have any trouble. Chances are, it won't cost you a cent, anyhow, for as I say, boundaries are plenty loose and for the most part written records don't exist at all. This country is brand new and it will be years before courts are set up and actual records filed according to law. I'd say take what you want and wait for the rest to catch up, else somebody may beat you to it.'

Leaving the stage station, Jeff said to Soapy and Sling, 'I'm making a call farther up town. No need of you boys feeling you have to trail along. You see how quiet things are.'

Soapy shook his head. 'So's a panther when it's waiting to pounce. Sling and me are sticking around. We won't interfere.'

Seeing that it was useless to argue further, Jeff bent his steps for the Sharpe home. Soapy and Sling squatted at their ease under the oaks and Jeff knocked at the door. Aunt Amanda opened it, exclaiming when she saw him.

'Young man, you shouldn't be running loose. You should be keeping out of sight at Lizzie Jackson's hotel.'

Jeff smiled. 'The *Flame of Sunset* is in and I have friends guarding my back trail.' He jerked his head toward Soapy and Sling. 'So, I've come to thank both you and Debbie for your kindness.'

'Hum!' murmured Amanda Sharpe, her eyes twinkling. 'Well, you might as well come in.'

The house was in considerable disorder. Rugs were bundled up and crates of furniture stood about. Amanda Sharpe said, 'We are preparing to move.' She saw the quick dismay in Jeff's eyes and the twinkle deepened. 'Not back to Boston. To San Francisco. My brother has decided to get out of the river boating business. It—ah—is a trifle too strenuous. There is an opportunity in the import and export trade in San Francisco which is too good to miss. So he is taking advantage of it. We are leaving on the *River Queen* tomorrow afternoon. I'll tell Debbie that you are here.'

Aunt Amanda scurried away and presently Debbie came into the room. Jeff's pulse quickened. She was in gingham and charmingly girlish. Her manner was shy and reserved. Her first words were almost the same as her aunt had used. 'You shouldn't be moving around like this, Jeff Kennett.'

Jeff smiled. 'The town is very quiet and I wasn't made to be caged up. Besides, I had to see you and your aunt and thank you for all you've done. And now I find you preparing to move. I'm glad I came before you did.'

He marked the soft sheen of her hair, the tender curves of the mouth and chin. He took a quick step forward, 'Debbie, I had to come half way across a continent to find you. And now—'

She stopped him with a quick little gesture. 'Please Jeff. I think—I know what you are about to say. And I don't want you to say it. I'm asking you not to. Please—!'

Jeff was stunned and shaken. He was

remembering how this girl had come into his arms that night out under the oaks, how her lips had rested warm on his own. He was remembering that she, along with her aunt, had dared much in aiding his escape from the mob. So he had allowed himself to think—to dream a little. And now—!

She saw the bewilderment in his eyes, saw in his face that same stern and craggy look he had shown at the time of the stage holdup. 'There are things—you don't understand, Jeff,' she pleaded. 'I know I gave you reason to think—It was shameless of me—But now—'

'No, I don't understand,' said Jeff slowly. 'I was figuring on a ranch, somewhere along the river, where those deep, rich plains run down. I was going to keep five hundred head of my best cattle to start with on that ranch. I've been thinking of all I—we—could do, and of the empire we could build with a start like that. I'd build you the finest ranch-house in all California, and—'

She said again, stiffly, almost woodenly, 'There are things you cannot know, Jeff. Please—!'

A sort of cynical weariness showed in Jeff's face. His voice was harsh. 'All right,' he agreed. 'I'll just forget the ranch idea. Seems there is something I hadn't thought of, for a fact. Which is that a Texas cowboy shouldn't be aspiring to the hand of a daughter of the

Sharpe family—from Boston. Any man is a fool to dream. Well, I guess this is it. Good-bye.'

He turned and went to the door. She made no effort to stop him. Her voice was very small and choked as she whispered, 'Good-bye, Jeff.'

The door closed behind him and Debbie Sharpe gave a soft little wail, dropped her face in her hands and began to sob. But Jeff did not know that. All he knew was that the world had turned bleak and gray, and that Soapy and Sling were on their feet, a poised alertness about them, their eyes turned in the direction of the river.

'Some shootin' down there,' growled Soapy. 'We just heard it. We better be getting down that way, Jeff.'

'It's a wild town,' answered Jeff, his thoughts still locked on other things. 'Bound to be shooting of some sort, now and then.'

Soapy rolled his gaunt shoulders. 'I got a feelin'. Let's get down there.'

They headed back for the riverfront and presently saw groups of excited men talking and milling. Soapy stopped one of them. 'What's all the ruckus, partner?' he asked.

'Shooting scrape in the Eagle,' was the answer. 'Shag Taggart put another notch on his gun.'

The name jerked Jeff back to the full import of the moment. 'Who did Taggart smoke it out with?' he demanded.

'Dunno. I just heard it said that Taggart was in the mix and that he came off with a whole skin, while the other feller didn't.'

They hurried toward the Eagle. There was a big jam of men in front of the place and Jeff and his two riders had some difficulty in pushing their way into the saloon. Here the jam was even tighter, but Jeff, urged on by a queer hunch, elbowed and shoved and finally broke into the clear, just in time to see a couple of men about to lift a limp figure from the floor.

Jeff said, his voice brittle and harsh, 'Let him be. He's a friend of ours. We'll take care of him.'

The limp figure was Harry Travers, and it needed only a glance to show that he was dead. He had been shot in the back.

★   ★   ★

There was a raw, savage tension in the air, but finally two miners, stunned and subdued by the killing, offered to help. Jeff directed them to carry the body of Harry Travers down to the *Flame of Sunset*, and sent Sling along to show the way. Then, with Soapy keeping a cold and narrowed eye on the rest of the room, he faced the bartender across the mahogany. In his hand he held the silver-mounted six-shooter Amanda Sharpe had given him.

'All right,' said Jeff harshly. 'You must have seen it. What happened—and how? If you don't give it to me straight, you'll never speak another word, for I'll blow the whole top off your head. I mean business, mister. Speak up!'

The bartender licked his lips. 'Travers—Travers was standing—watching a poker game. Taggart came in, saw him, went for his cutter. He—he shot Travers twice. Travers spun around—and—while he was going down—pulled a derringer and tried for Taggart—but missed. That—that's all.'

'Not all,' Jeff growled. 'Where'd Taggart go?'

Again the bartender licked his lips. He jerked his head weakly toward a rear door. 'Back—back there!'

Jeff knew then that the fellow had told the truth. He prowled toward the door, gun poised and ready. Over his shoulder he said, 'Watch 'em, Soapy.'

He tried the door. It was not locked. Crouched a trifle, every nerve end tingling with alertness, he jerked the door open. Before him a stairway rose to the second story of the building. It was full of dusky shadow and Jeff paused a moment while his eyes adjusted to the change of light. Then he went up the stairs, slowly, carefully, testing each step before putting his full weight on it.

In spite of this care, the stairs creaked complainingly. At the top of them a rectangle of pale light showed, like the entrance to a hall of some sort. Jeff, his eyes fixed on that rectangle of light, went on up.

The hall was about twenty feet in length and at the far end a dusty, cob-webbed window let in the filtered daylight. Beyond the head of the stairs, on either hand, were two rows of closed doors. The question was, which of those rooms held Shag Taggart?

It was ticklish going. Shooting, when and if it came would be at close quarters, and deadly. Jeff couldn't afford to make any mistakes. He knew that Taggart, listening, would have heard the creaking of the stairs and would know that the cautious approach boded no good for him. The man would be set like a hair trigger. If Jeff went into one of those rooms and found it empty, Taggart might be waiting for him in the hall when he came out, with all the advantage. And if Taggart was in the room Jeff picked to enter, he would still have the advantage as Jeff tried to come in.

It was as dangerous a spot as Jeff had ever been in and the tension laid fine sweat across his face. Then Jeff remembered that Harry Travers had been shot in the back. That was the sort Shag Taggart was—that kind of killer. If Taggart thought and acted along those lines—! The gleam in Jeff's eyes deepened. It was a trick worth trying.

He turned and began going along the hall backward, letting his boot heels down, not too loudly, but loudly enough for the sound to carry to any of the rooms along the hall. He made a sound like a man pacing the length of the hall, slowly, but with a deliberate purpose, and like a man looking ahead, but not behind. Only, Jeff wasn't looking ahead. He was facing the head of the stairs and gambling that a renegade who had shot one man in the back would try that same trick on another.

The tension now was like a chill pain. Then suddenly Jeff's straining ears picked up the faintest flutter of sound, back toward the stairs. A door was opening, very softly and cautiously.

Jeff went down on one knee, close to the wall on his left. He was just in time, for abruptly a burly figure lunged from the door to the left of the head of the stairs. Gunflame spurted in crimson blobs and the narrow hallway seemed to spread and creak under the bellowing thunder of the report. Glass tinkled and fell from the window. Shag Taggart was shooting as fast as he could, lacing the hall with lead, blindly certain that he would catch his man before he could turn. But Taggart's lead was high and to one side of Jeff's crouched figure. And Jeff, pushing his gun level, drove in a single answering shot, carefully centered. He heard the animal-like grunt of shock that burst from Taggart's lips. He saw Taggart's dark bulk weave and stagger and let him have it again. Taggart fell backwards and rolled, limp and slumped, down the stairs.

Jeff went down after him, gun ready for another shot, if another shot was needed. But it was not. Taggart had rolled half through the door at the bottom of the stairs, quite lifeless. Jeff stepped over him as he moved out into the main saloon. Soapy, strained and tense, relaxed. 'You,' he said to Jeff, 'are making an old man out of me.'

The bartender had not yet left. Soapy had held him in the place along with the rest. Now Jeff turned to the fellow. 'You can go back to your job. Taggart will never bother you or anyone else again.'

The barkeep, licking his lips, was staring at the huddled figure of Shag Taggart. He shrugged and mumbled, 'Either way, I'm out of a job. Taggart owned this joint, though few knew it.'

Jeff turned to the others. 'Anybody got any questions to ask, any quarrel to take up?' he demanded curtly. 'No? Fair enough. Come on, Soapy.'

All stood aside to let them pass. These tall, lean men, with the stain of Texas wind and sun in their faces, were plainly not to be trifled with. Until this time, Shag Taggart had been the big bully boy of the town. Now Shag Taggart was dead, and there was a look about the man who had killed him that none wished to challenge.

CHAPTER ELEVEN

Captain Bill Ballinger met them at the gangplank. His face was bitter. 'Well?' he growled.

'Taggart is dead,' said Jeff briefly.

'High time,' said Bill. 'Harry Travers was a good man—a good friend. Taggart was laying for him, I guess, because Harry took care of that worthless swab who tried to burn up the *Flame* on us. We'll do the best we can by Harry. Andy McLain is making a coffin. I'm wondering where Harry would like it best.'

Jeff waved a hand across the river. 'Out there somewhere, under one of those big oaks. A man could ask no sweeter place to rest.'

So it was done, in the soft, late afternoon, with the light of the autumn sunset spreading ruddy across the tawny plains. They mounded the grave smoothly and evenly, put up a simple head board and went away.

Said Bill Ballinger, 'I'm not forgetting that Noah Carlin is just as much responsible as was Taggart.'

'Nor I,' Jeff Kennett replied. 'Noah Carlin is one more man I lock horns with, final and complete, before I head back for Texas.'

Captain Bill swung an alert head. 'What kind of talk is that? Going back to Texas, I mean. For it has been in my mind all along, lad—that this country was to be your country, from now on. It is new country, rich, fine and free, and it needs men like you. You're not thinking what you are saying.'

Jeff said harshly, 'It can get along without me, and I can get along without it. Texas is where I belong. I understand the people back there—and I don't here. Not all of them.'

Captain Bill did not argue, but several times his glance, serious and troubled, rested on Jeff. Later that evening, when they had finished a gloomy supper in the ship's cabin, Bill stoked his pipe, got up and began pacing back and forth in the ship's cabin. 'I'm going to have my say, lad,' he growled, 'and you're going to listen to me. I've watched you, Jeff Kennett, watched you standing there on the deck, your eyes fixed on country running out from the river, and I've seen the dreams in your eyes and known what they mean. You see a ranch out in those plains, a ranch so big a man can scarce measure its limits. You see cattle, great herds of them, grazing and fattening, drinking at the water courses, or at the river itself, and you see them lazing and resting in the shade of the oaks through the warm summer days. That's a good dream, lad—a fine dream—and one you can make come true, and be happy over. And then there are those men of yours, and fine men they are, too. Maybe they have dreams and they need you to help make them real. I doubt they're wanting to go back to Texas. Is it asking too much that you do something for them?'

Jeff Kennett made no reply.

'I—ah well, 'tis a poor convincer I am, perhaps,' the captain continued. 'But I know there is deep truth in what I'm trying to tell you. And,' here a sly twinkle came into Captain Bill's eyes, 'I know that the ways of the feminine mind have bedeviled many a man before this, and also that in the end a woman follows her heart, though her mind be a capricious thing. A man must have patience to gather in the best things of life. And now I'll mind my tongue.'

Again Jeff Kennett said nothing, but got up and left the cabin. He squatted on his heels, his back against the pilot house and smoked endless cigarettes as he stared off into the velvety night. Hours later he came back to the cabin and found Captain Bill already snoring in his bunk.

Climbing into his own bunk, Jeff smiled grimly. 'You may be a poor convincer, Bill Ballinger,' he murmured. 'But you make a man think—plenty!'

* * *

The *Flame of Sunset* met the cattle miles below Red Bluff. Buck Yarnell and Stony Peters and the rest of the crew had kept the herd at a steady but leisurely drift down river as Jeff had instructed them to, and the animals were fat and sleek from the lush grazing along the river meadows.

Captain Bill maneuvered a sound berthing against the bank and the heavy loading gangplank was run out. Jeff called the riders all about him and said, 'We're saving five hundred of the best breeding stock, boys. Keep that in mind when you cut out the critters for this loading.'

'What's the idea?' asked Buck Yarnell. 'You figerin' on startin' up a new ranch, Jeff?'

'Just that, Buck. Wait until you get a good look at the plains, lower down. You never saw grazing land like it. You boys won't have to dig gold for a living, in case you want to stay on out here.'

Buck's old eyes gleamed. 'That's what I call good news. Me, I'm gettin' too durned old to ride plumb back to Texas. And I never was that crazy after gold that I'd bust my back diggin' for it. You boys hear that? We're goin' to set up a ranch, Texas style, in this here country and watch it grow. Yessir, that sure is good news.'

They labored and sweated and loaded the *Flame* and barge to capacity. Then, as Captain Bill was about to cast off, Jeff went over to him, smiling grimly. 'You'll have to make another trip without me, Bill. I'll send Soapy and Sling along to take care of the cattle, but I'm staying over. Buck Yarnell and I got some riding and looking to do. A man doesn't pick a new ranch out of virgin territory every day of his life, and I want to make sure that my first choice is the right one.'

Captain Bill hit Jeff a joyous, open handed buffet between the shoulders. 'Time you came to your senses,' he rumbled happily. 'You take care of that new ranch, and I'll take care of the cattle.'

★   ★   ★

The next morning Jeff and Buck Yarnell were up and riding before the sun came over the Sierras. They forded the river and struck off south and west, gradually swinging further and further away from the river until its course was only a line of green timber in the far distance. The great tawny plains swept way on every hand, and under foot the hoofs of their horses padded on sun-cured grass so deep and matted it seemed to muffle all sound. Jeff heard Buck Yarnell mutter again and again in his amazement and appreciation of possibilities of such land.

Once, when they reined in to look around, old Buck said, 'I had to grow old and grizzled before I looked on country that was a cattleman's heaven, younker. Who ever saw such graze before? Who ever did?'

All about them as they rode, myriads of tiny grass finches and the larger, more colorful meadow larks lifted and floated on careless wings. Long eared jack-rabbits scudded out of their path, and as they rode up to one side of a small grove of valley oaks, a herd of antelope burst out the far side.

They came to a small, lazy watercourse, winding an indolent way toward the distant river. Covey after covey of valley quail whirred up on all sides, and every languid pool held a quota of mallard ducks, fat and heavy as they lifted with protesting quacking into the air, their plumage bright and beautiful in the sunlight.

Buck Yarnell spoke again. 'This land loves life, younker. And life loves the land. The Lord was plumb generous when He made this Californy.'

Jeff Kennett nodded. He spoke softly, as though to himself. 'Captain Bill was right. I was foolish to ever think of going back. From now on, this is my country.'

They let their horses drink at the

watercourse, then crossed and rode on. In time another wide grove of oaks appeared ahead, and when they had drawn closer, Jeff Kennett abruptly reined in, his silver gray eyes fixed and slightly narrowed.

'Smoke lifting above those oaks, Buck—and some movement there. We're no longer alone out here. What do you think? Do we turn back or go ahead?'

Grizzled old Buck made a long survey. 'We're aiming to set up a ranch somewhere through here,' he said presently. 'Now is as good a time as any to find out what kind of neighbors we may have.'

Jeff nodded. 'Come on.'

They rode forward with an instinctive wariness that heeded everything and missed nothing. And as the distance lessened they saw that their approach had indeed been observed. Figures of men were moving about under the trees, but Jeff and Buck were still too far away to tell whether those men were red or white. Then, as they drew closer, they saw that both white men and red were there, drawn up in a line at the edge of the grove, awaiting their further approach.

'They're missin' nothin' about us, younker, but they're not exactly hostile,' murmured Buck Yarnell. 'I think we can talk to these men.'

'I think so,' agreed Jeff. 'We'll see.'

He threw up his right arm, palm open and

facing forward, in the peace sign as old as the plains themselves, and one of the white men moved out a few paces from the trees, an arm lifting in an answering peace salute.

Jeff and Buck closed in to within a few yards and Jeff said quietly, 'Howdy, friend. I hope my partner and me are not riding forbidden trails?'

The man smiled. 'Don Carlos might say that you were. But not I, John Sutter. My Indians are preparing the midday repast. You are welcome to partake with me.'

There was a strange, old world courtesy in this man's manner and words which was utterly convincing. Jeff Kennett dismounted and held out his hand. 'Glad to know you, John Sutter. I am Jefferson Kennett. This is my trail boss, Buck Yarnell.'

The hand clasp was strong and warm. At one time, Jeff Kennett judged, this John Sutter must have been an immensely strong and vigorous man. Now the strongly determined face was drawn and seamed, the blue eyes shadowed with some deep trouble, and the hair above the broad, thinker's brow had turned to snow. Such was John Sutter, one of the great and vital forces in the early fortunes and development of the new Californian empire.

Jeff and Buck knew that John Sutter was judging them, measuring them. He said slowly, 'Trail boss. That suggests cattle. For some time now stories have been coming to me of a great herd of cattle that have come across the northern passes and down through Lassen Meadows. Some of these cattle, it is said, have already been taken to San Francisco by boat. The word is that these cattle came clear from Texas, a stupendous achievement by the men who drive them, if true.'

'It is true,' said Jeff. 'The herd is mine. My men and I left Texas with that herd over two years ago.'

A quick gleam shone in John Sutter's eyes. 'Tremendous!' he said. 'Tremendous! Gentlemen, I am happy that our trails have crossed. We shall have much to talk about. Come! While we dine, you shall tell me about that drive.'

In all, some twenty men made up John Sutter's group. Most of these were Indians, squat, quiet, placid-faced fellows, obviously pastoral and unwarlike. They seemed to have a great affection for Sutter and in return his manner toward them was quiet and kindly. Besides Sutter himself, there were three other white men, older men, also obviously of a pastoral turn of mind and not infected with the virus of gold madness. In one corner of the grove was tethered a number of horses, both saddle and pack animals. Bedding and other equipment was spread around, and food for the meal was laid out on a sheet of canvas spread upon the ground.

'We have been here two days, waiting the arrival of Don Carlos,' John Sutter explained. 'He has agreed to meet me here for a discussion of matters vital to both of us. I understand that he is on his way and should arrive later today. Sit down, gentlemen, and eat. Our fare is simple, but there is plenty of it.'

Among other items of this spread of 'simple' fare was a whole antelope, roasted in a pit dug beside the grove. There were fat mallard ducks, crisply brown, swimming in their own juices. There were succulent greens and great loaves of brown crusted bread, and fruits and sweetmeats. A cask of wine, made from wild grapes, was close at hand, and a glass of it gave off all the tang and wild perfume of the parent fruit. It was a meal the equal of which Jeff and Buck had seldom seen.

The first keen edge of hunger removed, John Sutter looked at Jeff and said, 'Now that drive. Tell me about it.'

Jeff did so in a simple, matter-of-fact way, with no hint of heroics in the recital. Yet unknowingly he painted a picture in bold, raw colors and with strong, slashing brush strokes that was the more effective because of its straightforward simplicity. John Sutter listened in rapt, glowing attention and when Jeff had finished, sighed deeply.

'An epic,' he said gravely. 'I would like to have been part of it. The herd, you intend marketing all of it in San Francisco?'

Jeff shook his head. 'Not all. I am keeping five hundred head of the best breeding stock to start a ranch somewhere on these plains. That is why Buck and I are riding today. We are looking for a site for that ranch.'

Sutter nodded, smiling faintly to himself. 'It was my guess that something of the sort was in your mind, and California needs more men with the same idea, instead of these senseless hordes with their all consuming mania for gold—gold. They cannot see that the real and lasting wealth of this country is the earth and what it will nourish and grow. No, they cannot see that. And in their madness for the flecks of yellow metal they see in their sluices and rockers and pans, they gouge and rip, plunder and despoil, loot and destroy. They fill our sparkling streams with mud and silt, they scar the clean hills, they lie and cheat and steal and kill, all for the sake of a few ounces of that mocking metal, metallic gold. They sell their souls for it—the fools!'

John Sutter had started quietly, softly, but now his eyes were flashing, and there was in him the great bitterness of a man who had been wronged and wronged again by his heedless, clamoring fellows. 'I am sorry if I have spoken in what may seem to you an unchristian manner, gentlemen,' he went on, apologetically. 'But I have suffered much, much at the hands of these gold seekers. I was here early—long before men ever dreamed that there was gold to be found in the foot-hills. The possibilities were here and it was my dream to make this country a paradise on earth, where man might find the peace and contentment and plenty he had striven to find through all the ages. I built and I planted and for a time I prospered. I treated the Indians kindly and in return they became great and good friends. For a time that paradise was here—right in this great valley.

'Then came the ill fated day of discovery of gold. The word spread and the madness started. Men left my employ, left the tilling of the good and gracious earth and joined the stampede. Only a few, a very few, faithful ones remained with me. I had herds of cattle, but these the gold seekers went at like wolves, stealing and slaughtering for food. They grew nothing, created nothing. They just consumed, consumed, like a horde of ravening insects. When the wagon trains began to come in from across the plains, they turned their ox teams into my standing wheat, to feed and trample and waste. They brought nothing, they took everything. First my cattle and my produce—now my lands. Gentlemen, I am a religious man. But I curse the evil day when James Marshall found the first gold at Coloma. It has destroyed my dream—and it was a good dream as well as a great dream.'

The fire was gone out of John Sutter, now. His chin had dropped on his chest and he stared with brooding eyes at nothing. Suddenly he was old and very tired.

Buck Yarnell cleared his throat. 'Why didn't you fight them off, friend? Back home we have prime medicine for a cow thief. We string him up to the nearest tree. We let no man steal our cattle or trample our grass.'

John Sutter swung a weary head. 'I am a man of peace. Men like me need the law to protect their rights. And there is no law, yet. Once or twice my Indians tried to object, to defend what was mine—and theirs. They were shot down like dogs.'

'I am looking for land to start a ranch on, yes,' Jeff Kennett said slowly. 'But I don't intend or want to steal it. I am willing to pay a fair price.' He waved a hand. 'This land hereabouts, who owns it, Mr. Sutter?'

'At one time I believed that I did,' answered John Sutter. 'It is part of a grant made to me by Don Carlos. But now questions as to the authenticity of that grant have arisen. That is why I am here today, at this spot, and why I have arranged another meeting with Don Carlos. I would ask him to give me the document of proof of that grant.

But,' and here that ghost of a bitter smile touched his lips again, 'it seems that Don Carlos has suddenly developed a shrewdness, a bargaining turn of mind that may make things difficult. I have it on fairly reliable authority that the Don intends to strike a hard bargain and demand a payment for that document which may be beyond my ability to meet without making a pauper of myself. You see, the gold and the greed for it have touched him, too.'

'But he once made this grant to you, of his own will and in good faith?' asked Jeff.

'Oh, yes. I had done him a small favor, not with the idea of being rewarded, you understand. I just happened to be at the right spot—at the right time, you might say.'

'What was—this small favor, Mr. Sutter?'

'It was in the earlier days. Don Carlos' son, Pico, in company with a number of other young hot heads, were bent on organizing an attack on the topographical expedition led by Fremont, then a lieutenant. Fremont was headstrong in those days; he made some enemies. At any rate, the attack amounted to little enough, with no casualties on either side, and young Pico alone was captured. I managed to prevail on Fremont and kept him from hanging Pico as an example. Pico was freed and went back to his father. For that, Don Carlos made this land grant to me.'

'And now wants to crawl out of the deal, eh?' growled Buck Yarnell.

John Sutter shrugged. 'Shall we put it—that he wishes to bargain?'

'The slippery whelp!' exploded old Buck. 'What he needs is a good booting around. And I'd enjoy being the hombre that swung the boot. How about it, Jeff?'

Jeff Kennett's silver gray eyes held a cool gleam. 'He needs something of the kind, for a fact.'

Sutter laughed softly. 'I like your fierce independence,' he said. 'It is refreshing. Perhaps if you sit beside me during the discussion, Don Carlos may be, shall we call it, a trifle more lenient?'

'We'll sit,' growled Buck. 'And he better be, or I'll wring his neck.'

John Sutter laughed again and lifted his glass. 'To the happy circumstance of our meeting, gentlemen! I am, frankly, fearful of my own future in this country. Somehow I feel things slipping away from me. But men like you hold the future in your hands. Your idea of a ranch is good and sound. I like it, and I have in mind the perfect place. Later, I will show it to you, and it shall be yours, without cost or favor. In a way it will be the fruition of at least a part of my dream, to see great herds grazing in content and plenty on the bounty of this wonderful land.'

As they lowered their glasses an Indian

came with soft padding swiftness and murmured something to John Sutter, who nodded and got to his feet. He said, 'The party has been sighted. They will be here within minutes.'

CHAPTER TWELVE

The party numbered over a score. They rode magnificent horses and made a gaudy, colorful picture as they came up to the oak grove through the warm, clear sunlight. John Sutter, after issuing orders for the preparation of more food, went alone to meet the newcomers.

Jeff Kennett and Buck Yarnell stood at the fringe of the grove, watching. 'Plenty of shine and show, younker,' Buck growled. 'Calculated to make men kowtow, I reckon. They'll get none of it from me. What do you think of this man Sutter, anyhow?'

'A big man, Buck. Even a great man. But with one weakness. He doesn't like force. And no frontier was ever met and held without a little force applied in the right spot at the right time.'

The newcomers now dismounted, turning their horses over to the care of Sutter's Indians, and with these their manner was haughty, almost contemptuous. A place apart was provided for the vaqueros to eat, and only Don Carlos and two others joined John Sutter at the tarpaulin spread on the ground. Sutter caught the eye of Jeff Kennett and Jeff and Buck prowled over. Sutter made the introductions.

'Don Carlos, his son, Don Pico, and his nephew, Don Luis. And these are my new and good friends, Jefferson Kennett and Buck Yarnell. I am sorry, Don Carlos, that we have already dined, but I did not expect your arrival until toward evening. However, we will have a glass of wine with you.'

It was plain that the newcomers looked upon Jeff and Buck as little better than Sutter's Indians. Jeff's eyes narrowed, while old Buck growled very softly in his throat, like some grizzled old wolf picking up the first thread of hostile scent on a vagrant breeze.

Don Carlos himself was a squat, thick set man, with a definite paunch and the shine of sweat across his broad, rather stupid features. Don Pico was a younger replica of his father, while Don Luis was of slimmer build. He ate and drank with a sort of feline daintiness and an almost affected indolence.

John Sutter got down to business almost immediately, but without a great deal of success. The talk was all in Spanish and only by tone and the looks on the faces of the men could Jeff and Buck get some idea of how the discussion was progressing. But they saw that it was not going in John Sutter's favor.

Don Carlos put on a great show of shrugging and turning up palms, while greed and avarice lay naked in his rather small, black eyes. From time to time Don Pico put in a word or two, but Don Luis said nothing, seeming fully occupied with a catlike picking over of the food. Jeff and Buck were finally convinced that Don Carlos was playing with John Sutter as a cat would with a mouse, enjoying the fact that he had Sutter where he wanted him, that he held the whip hand and could and would use it. Into his manner and words a certain contempt began to creep, and it was also mirrored in the eyes of the two younger men.

That John Sutter felt that contempt showed in the deepening color in his face. But so held was he by the belief that it was possible to reason with any man, once the proper approach was discovered, that he kept on trying to reach his middle ground long after Jeff and Buck were taut with anger. Finally John Sutter made what was evidently a last offer and to that Don Carlos shook his head and smiled smugly.

John Sutter turned to Jeff and said quietly, 'It is as I feared. He wants everything. He would pauperize me in return for ground I would be too poor to utilize. I have used every argument at my command.'

'No!' said Jeff. 'You've failed to use the only one these fellows will understand, Mr. Sutter. Will you let me speak and pass along my words to them?'

John Sutter shrugged. 'Why not? I have nothing more to lose.'

'Good!' rapped Jeff. He turned his eyes on Don Pico. 'They were going to hang you, weren't they?' he said. 'They would have hung you. But John Sutter stepped in and saved your worthless life.' Jeff swung his glance now to the startled Don Carlos. 'And you, in what you called gratitude—you made a land grant to John Sutter. But you didn't mean it—and now you would bargain and attempt the ruin of the man who saved your son's life. You ride and move and talk with arrogance as though you were a man of honor and superior to other men. You don't know what honor means!'

Jeff's tone and manner told much, but when John Sutter gave the words honest interpretation, Don Carlos recoiled with a snarl and Pico jumped to his feet. It was Don Luis who surprised, however. Lithe as a cat, he lunged across at Jeff, plucking a knife from the gaudy sash about his waist. Jeff promptly hit him a back-handed smash across the face which knocked him end over end. Then there was a gun in Jeff's hand, the muzzle pointing squarely at the middle of Don Carlos' protuberant, quivering belly.

'Hold them down!' barked Jeff. 'Keep them quiet, or you get it, Don Carlos! I mean business!'

Don Carlos did not need John Sutter to interpret these words. The way that gun bore steadily at his middle and the cold light in the silver gray eyes of the man who held it told Don Carlos everything he needed to know. He mumbled a command at his son and a harsher one at Don Luis, who was crawling shakily to his feet, wiping the blood from his bruised lips and glaring at Jeff with murderous malevolence.

At Jeff's shoulder, Buck Yarnell drew his gun and growled, 'Hah! Now we're getting down to cases. Make him fork over that document to John Sutter. He's sure to have it along with him, figuring he held the whip hand and could force Sutter to put everything on the line.'

'I'm going to,' said Jeff. He fixed his glance on Don Carlos, but he spoke to John Sutter. 'You know what price you could pay him, what you would pay him without feeling that you had been cheated too badly. Tell him that you will pay him that much, and not one penny more. And tell him to fork over that document, deed, bill of sale, or whatever it is.'

John Sutter hesitated. 'But that is duress. I do not like to do business that way.'

'It is the only way you can do business

with this hombre. You're not cheating him, Mr. Sutter. You are just making sure that he doesn't cheat you. When you deal with rascals, you write your own rules, or they will write theirs. Tell him to hand over that document and that you will pay him only what the land is worth, no more. When you do that, you are in the clear.'

John Sutter sighed deeply and gave the words to Don Carlos, who recoiled as if he had been stung. His mouth opened to a volley of shrill protestations, but these broke off sharply as Jeff leaned a trifle closer and made a stabbing move with his gun. 'Hand it over,' he said harshly.

The look in Jeff's eyes—and the gun—got results. Don Carlos fumbled in his sash, brought out a roll of parchment and dropped it on the canvas. Jeff scooped it up with his free hand, gave it to John Sutter.

'Look it over and see if this is it.'

Sutter unrolled the parchment and nodded. 'Yes, this is what I wanted. But the method—'

'Is the kind that is understood in any language,' cut in Buck Yarnell. 'Don't worry about the method, Mr. Sutter. It gets results.'

John Sutter said, still troubled, 'I hold the title now. But do I keep it? They outnumber us heavily, they are all armed, while there is but a single gun in my whole party, used merely to provide meat. Long before we can get back to the river and cross it to safety, they can surround us and wipe us out.'

'I've got the answer to that, too,' said Jeff. 'In the first place, Buck and I got guns—and know how to use them. In the second, we take Don Carlos with us, well toward the river, while he orders his crowd to pack up and get out, back the way they came. When we are beyond any chance of their coming back at us, Don Carlos will be freed to return to them. But if they try any devilment before that time, Don Carlos gets the first slug where it will do the most good. Explain that to him, and then get your men to making ready to leave.'

'And,' suggested Buck Yarnell, 'just to put a snapper to that whip, tell him that Jeff and me are Texicans, who've been over tougher jumps than this, many a time.'

John Sutter told Don Carlos, told him slowly and distinctly. Don Carlos licked his lips and glared murder, but he nodded slowly to show he understood. Then as John Sutter hurried off to tell his Indians and others to make ready to depart, Jeff gave a little wave to his gun. 'Over here, Don Carlos,' he ordered. 'Over here away from all the rest, where Buck and I can keep an eye on you. Won't do you any good to scowl and mutter. You brought this on yourself.'

Don Carlos obeyed, then gave orders to

Pico and Luis. Pico hurried away, but Luis stood there, dabbing at his puffed lips, his eyes black with hate. He held a rapid fire argument with Don Carlos over something to which Don Carlos seemed to object for a time, then finally shrugged acquiescence. A hot triumph shone in Don Luis' eyes.

'Up to some kind of deviltry, Jeff,' growled Buck. 'Hold 'em both here and make them say all that again with John Sutter to listen in.'

Jeff nodded and, when Sutter came back, said, 'These two seemed to agree on something while you were gone, Mr. Sutter. Suggest that they say it again.'

To Sutter's questioning, Don Carlos spouted words and the anxious look in Sutter's eyes deepened. He shook his head, shook it again, and answered Don Carlos sharply.

'Come on, John Sutter,' said Jeff. 'Buck and I want to know. What's on their minds?'

'A ridiculous thing,' said Sutter. 'Don Luis, yonder, says that his honour was smirched when you struck him. He challenges you to fight him—with knives. Not to be considered, of course. Pay no heed to them.'

Somewhere Don Luis had picked up a single word in English. He spoke it now, with decided accent, but intelligibly enough, and doubly so because of the sneer that accompanied it.

'Coward,' he said, then repeated the word. 'Coward!'

The chill in Jeff Kennett's eyes turned to simmering fire. 'Tell him,' he rasped harshly, 'that he's bought himself a fight. Tell him that, John Sutter!'

'No!' exclaimed Sutter in startled agitation. 'No, I won't hear of it. Don Luis has a reputation along that line. He has killed several men in knife duels. I won't hear of it!'

Growled Buck Yarnell, 'Was it guns, I'd say go ahead, younker. But knives—I dunno—I dunno—'

'Coward!' sneered Don Luis again.

'Knives, guns, anything,' Jeff said hoarsely. 'He's asked for it. Don't you see, Buck, how it is? We aim to set up a ranch in these parts. Should I back down from that sneering whelp, they'd have us all tagged as a bunch of yellow coyotes. I've never been in a knife fight, but I've seen 'em and know something about how to handle myself. I'm fighting him. Tell him that, Sutter. Tell him!'

John Sutter knew it was useless to argue further. He shrugged, shook his head sadly and spoke to Don Carlos. At the words a red cunning shone in the latter's eyes, while Don Luis spread his battered lips in a cruel smile.

'Buck,' Jeff said, 'I'm leaving Don Carlos in your care. You know what you're to do if you have to.'

'I know, and I will,' Buck promised. He dropped a gnarled hand on Don Carlos' shoulder, jerked him to one side and stabbed a gun muzzle against his spine. 'If any tricks show,' he rumbled, 'your backbone comes apart, pronto.'

'We'll need room,' said Jeff curtly. 'So we'll move out past the trees. And I'll need a knife.'

Now Don Pico came hurrying back and Don Luis spoke to him. Pico turned, stared at Jeff and laughed. Jeff flexed his arms.

'I'll fight that whelp too, if he wants it. Tell him so, John Sutter. But tell him right now I need a knife to work on that sneering cousin of his.'

When John Sutter spoke, Pico jerked a knife from his sash and threw it at Jeff's feet. Jeff picked it up, balanced it. It was razor sharp. Jeff locked his lean hand about the grip and jerked his head. 'Let's get this thing over with.'

Don Luis had recovered his own knife and, as the group moved out beyond the edge of the grove of trees, sent the weapon spinning into the air, catching it dexterously as it came down. Word, meanwhile, had spread through the grove and both John Sutter's Indians and Don Carlos' vaqueros came out to the fringe of the trees to watch. The vaqueros had apparently learned from

Pico of what had befallen their leader and they were openly menacing and sullen.

Buck Yarnell ground the muzzle of his gun a little deeper into Don Carlos' fat back. 'Just to be sure, you better remind that crowd of yours to stay put and play pretty,' he growled. John Sutter translated and Don Carlos called shrilly at the vaqueros, who gave back a little and nodded their understanding.

All eyes now centered on the two combatants who had already begun to circle round and round, crouching a trifle. Jeff Kennett held his blade pointing forward, as if it were a small, short sword, while Don Luis held his knife so the blade showed from the heel of his clenched hand. As he circled and circled, gradually drawing closer to Jeff, he made little weaving motions with the knife, until it flashed in the sun like the swaying of a snake's head, poised to strike.

Abruptly Don Luis darted in, crouched so low it seemed he almost flattened himself on the ground, and swung a wicked, back-handed slash that was calculated to rip a man's body wide open. Buck Yarnell, as he glimpsed the move, groaned slightly, almost closed his eyes. But he let out his breath in a relieved hiss as he saw Jeff sway clear of that scythe-like sweep of steel, then drive his own long arm forward.

Don Luis whirled away at the finish of his

stroke, but not fast enough to come entirely clear. Jeff's blade seemed barely to flick his adversary's left shoulder, but as Don Luis went on around, his gaudy shirt showed first a decided rip and then a quick spreading sogginess.

'You branded him, Jeff—you branded him!' whooped Buck.

Don Carlos paled. Pico's face showed concern and Don Luis, apparently recovering from his astonishment that in the first passage of arms he had been the one to feel the steel, began to circle again, faster than before. Again he darted in with that same low, whirling crouch, but this time his stroke with the knife was only a feint, for he shot out a hooking foot, calculated to cut Jeff's feet from under him. The maneuver came within an inch of succeeding. Jeff floundered, nearly fell and recovered barely in time as Don Luis came lunging back in, knife swung high for a driving, stabbing stroke.

But Jeff's left hand shot out and up, locked on Don Luis' wrist and held it there, while his own knife point pressed against the Don's throat. For a moment the tableau held, and it was apparent to every man watching that Jeff Kennett could cut the life from Don Luis right then and there, if he chose.

That Don Carlos thought he would was

plain, for the older man gave a bleating cry. The vaqueros groaned and Pico seemed struck numb. But Jeff Kennett did not drive his knife blade home. Instead, he reversed the weapon, drove the haft against Don Luis' face and with a hard shove knocked his man over backward.

Don Luis rolled over, scrambled to his feet, disheveled and pallid with fury. Without knowing it, Jeff had done Don Luis a worse injury than if he had cut his throat. He had made him look foolish and helpless. He had played with him, outmaneuvered him and then refused to kill him when he won the advantage.

This was something that Don Luis could never live down unless he wiped it out in blood, here and now. Throwing all caution to the winds, he came at Jeff in a fury slashing and striking. Jeff switched his knife to his left hand and drew his right back along his chest, that right hand knotting into a rock-hard fist, poised and waiting.

Evidently Don Luis and his supporters thought that Jeff's switching of his knife from right hand to left meant that in some way Jeff had injured that arm, for a new confidence shone red in Don Luis' eyes and his supporters cried their encouragement. Again and again Don Luis rushed in and each time Jeff slid away from him, on sure, prowling feet. And Don Luis, mad with frustration panted, 'Coward—coward!'

He rushed in again, driving his blade wickedly at Jeff's body. There was the clash of steel as Jeff caught the blade on his own and deflected the blow. And now Don Luis, off balance again, was the target Jeff had been waiting for. There came a powerful, rolling, snapping surge to Jeff's shoulders and that clenched and waiting right fist shot out. It caught Don Luis full in the center of his panting, snarling, hate-maddened face, and the impact was like the breaking of a board. The blow lifted Don Luis completely off his feet, turned him half over in the air and dropped him in a shuddering, senseless heap in the tawny grass. He lay there without a move.

Jeff tossed his knife contemptuously aside and turned to John Sutter. 'All right, we can leave now.'

Buck Yarnell half groaned, 'You doggoned idiot, you consarned crazy cub—why didn't you stick him? You had him dead to rights. Why didn't you stick him?'

'A knife,' growled Jeff, 'is dirty business. Them that like a knife can have it. I'll take my guns, or my fists. It's done with. That fellow is plumb convinced, I reckon. I say again, we'll leave now!'

CHAPTER THIRTEEN

They rode for an hour before John Sutter said, 'There is no further danger. We can let Don Carlos go. But I would speak to him, first.'

Sutter did speak to the sullen, but subdued Don Carlos. He spoke at length and though Jeff and Buck could not know the meaning of the words, they could tell by the tone that John Sutter was patiently trying to bring about some sort of satisfactory basis of understanding. It was equally plain that he was not succeeding. At length John Sutter shrugged resignedly. 'Very well. Let him go.'

'In a minute,' nodded Jeff. 'But first, tell him this. Tell him that he should know by this time that we mean business. Tell him we want no trouble with him in the future, but if he starts it, he and his crowd won't be handled very gently. Tell him that we are willing to pay our way, at a fair price, but if he buys a fight, it will be plenty of fight. Tell him that.'

But John Sutter's translation had no visible effect. 'All right,' growled Jeff in disgust. 'Tell him to git.'

Don Carlos left at a gallop, spurring his mount cruelly. Buck Yarnell said, 'We ain't through with that jigger. I got a hunch. He won't be satisfied until he gets his ears pinned back, proper. Yes, sir, I got a hunch.'

And John Sutter, staring after him, shook his head sadly. 'Too bad. I do not like to quarrel with any man. Until now I have found the Spanish dons to be kindly, courteous, friendly gentlemen, the souls of honor and integrity, even though many of them have suffered as much as I from depredations of the wilder elements among the goldseekers. They built up a gracious, hospitable culture across these fair lands, and I have enjoyed their friendship and valued it. Don Carlos was the only exception I knew.'

'There is always an exception,' said Jeff. 'I hope Don Carlos comes to his senses. A friend is to be desired above an enemy, any time.'

They rode on, swinging southeast. Always a fair, rich country lay ahead of them, warm and drowsing in the sunlight. They crossed another winding water-course, twisting a leisurely way toward the parent river and beyond this the plain seemed to rise slightly. In the far distance showed the green growth marking still another small creek. John Sutter reined in.

'This is the piece of land I had in mind for that ranch of yours, Jefferson Kennett,' he said. 'As you note, it lifts just a trifle higher than the plains surrounding, which is good for cattle when the rainy season comes. The grass is not quite so lush and coarse, but it is better quality and contains more nutriment. In the early days, before the influx of emigrants began to scatter and thin them out, I noted that the tule elk and the antelope foraged here a great deal by choice. And the wisdom of Nature's children is always sound. Here your cattle will find water on either hand, shelter under the oaks and graze reaching for miles between these two waterways and from the river clear back across the valley to the foothills in the west. What do you think of it?'

Jeff's eyes were gleaming as he followed the sweep of John Sutter's encompassing arm. Buck Yarnell murmured, 'Sounds good, looks good. Even to range limits easy to follow. This could be it, younker.'

'We'll look it over, Buck,' Jeff nodded. 'I like it. I like it a lot. But I want to be sure. Yeah, we'll look it over.'

John Sutter smiled. 'That is wise. I see you are eager to start exploring. So I will leave you to it. You will stop in at my fort and let me know your decision?'

'Yes,' said Jeff. 'And, if it is what I want, arrange payment with you.'

'There will be no payment, my young friend,' John Sutter smiled. 'As I said before, this will be a dream I am too old to fulfil of my own account. I will see the fruition of it through your youth and eagerness and industry. That will be payment enough. Until we meet again, then.'

John Sutter shook hands with them, then rode away with his Indians and other henchmen. Jeff and Buck began their exploration. They rode, all the rest of the day, then made a frugal camp for the night under an ancient oak, with the fragrant earth as their bed and with a ceiling of filtered starlight shining down through the patient, spreading crest above. All the next day they rode and in the soft dusk came back to the bank of the river. Here was a slight knoll with a grove of oak, looking down across the smooth sliding, amber waters.

Jeff Kennett said, 'Here will stand the headquarters, Buck. Right here on this knoll among the oaks. It is perfect. Every mile, every foot of it—perfect.'

Buck nodded a grizzled head. 'It is a queer feeling I have, younker. It is as though I've come—home.'

They turned back up river, found a ford in the early starlight where the channel narrowed to an easy swim for their horses. At midnight they came back to the bedded herd.

In the morning Jeff called his riders about him and told them all the story and their eyes shone with the promise of it. Buck Yarnell added his bit. 'Wait 'till you jiggers get a look at it. I'm telling you pilgrims—this is the promised land.'

Steadily they drifted the herd on down river, the days slow and warm and indolent behind the grazing cattle, the nights a time for eager discussion and planning about the campfire. And it was almost a surprise when, one midmorning, there came echoing from the river a series of whistle blasts, to signify that Captain Bill Ballinger and the *Flame of Sunset* were back.

Captain Bill tied up, sent out the gangplank and came ashore, grinning cheerfully. 'Cattle,' he boomed. 'Bring me cattle. Those San Francisco sports seem to like the flavor of Texas beef, Jeff. I've finagled a jump in price of five dollars a head on this next load.'

'Lucky day I found a man like you, Captain Bill,' said Jeff.

'Huh!' grunted Bill. 'I ain't had so much fun since I started river boating. Rather haul cattle than gold-crazy humans any time. Got better manners. How'd you come out on that ranch deal? Find what you want?'

Jeff's reply was so enthusiastic the riverman's chuckle deepened to a laugh. He reached for a pocket. 'Speaking of ranches reminds me. Here is something I'm to deliver to you.'

He held out a small sealed envelope. Across it, in feminine handwriting was written, 'Jefferson Kennett.' Jeff ripped it open, unfolded the enclosure and read:

> *Jefferson Kennett:*
> *Don't be a complete idiot. So many men are. So are some young women, who often say no when they mean yes, particularly when they set out to be martyrs because of a sadly bedraggled family pride. This is the advice of one who knows. Go right ahead with the plans for your ranch, and I will expect to see you in San Francisco.*
> *Amanda Sharpe*

Jeff folded the letter carefully and stowed it away. 'How'd you get ahold of this, Bill?' he demanded.

Bill shrugged, his eyes twinkling. 'It came aboard when I tied up at Sacramento for another load of fuel. Not bad news, I hope.'

'No,' said Jeff softly. 'Not bad news. Don't look so innocent. You know it's not bad news. But tell me—any trouble along the trip?'

'Not a smidgin. Not a sign of Noah Carlin or the *Gold Camp* anywhere. Keeps on like this, I'm going to be bored stiff. Well, what do you say—do we start loading?'

'We do. But first there is a job of parting out to do. I been waiting for Soapy and Sling to show up to help with the job.'

It took better than two days to finish the parting out job. When it was done with, five hundred cattle, the cream of the herd, were bunched and moved apart, taken upstream a little distance to a good ford, then sent splashing and swimming across to the west bank. As the last of the dripping cattle climbed out on the far side, Jeff turned to Buck Yarnell.

'Okay, old timer. I'm giving you four of the boys to trail this bunch to that promised land of ours. Soapy and Sling will be going down river again on the *Flame* and Stony Peters and the rest will take care of what's left of the herd on this bank. I doubt you'll have any trouble with Don Carlos before we get back for another load and by that time I'll be able to let you have a couple more men. If he does start anything, send one of your men after Stony and the others to help you out.'

The third trip down river was uneventful, though they were on continuous watch for any emergency, and Captain Bill had seen to it that there were guns enough aboard for every man on the *Flame*, in case of need. 'I'm not fooling around any more,' he said grimly. 'If Noah Carlin ever makes another try at river pirating, he won't meet up with just fists and brickbats. He'll run into hot lead and plenty of it. From here on out we fight for keeps.' But they saw no sign of the *Gold Camp*.

They did not stop at Sacramento, but

bustled right on with a whistle blast to announce their passing. They steamed the day out and on through the night, and, in the bright clear morning light, chugged past Rio Vista, where, at their whistle, Johnny Galway and his crew lined the rail of the *Antelope* to wave and yell.

Beyond Rio Vista they broke into wider waters, where the San Joaquin River, yellow and silt laden, came writhing down from the great southern valley, to mingle its waters with those of the Sacramento, in a waterway which pointed straight to the west. They ran out to where Suisan Bay opened on the north, backed by smooth and rounded hills, yellow gold in the sunlight.

South now they turned, and new dark heights rose beyond the soft curving foothills, then, straight ahead to the west, a powder blue, towering peak seemed to block their way. The rounded foothills began pinching in on either hand, narrower and narrower until the waterway seemed but a few hundred yards across, with the foothills lifting straight up from the water's edge. Then, just as it seemed they must be steaming into a pocket of some sort, fresh distance loomed ahead, and the waters widened and widened until the far shore to the north was lost in pale mist.

Steadily the *Flame of Sunset* drove on, and the sloping foothills kept pace on the left.

Finally these foothills ran out into a lowering point. The waterway led around that point and the course was south once more. To the west the hills closed in slightly, dark and green with timber and shrub, while islands, small and tufted, lifted ahead. White caps came chasing in before the breeze, to slap against the *Flame*'s bow and send little bursts of spray and spume flying.

Ahead lay a distinct, curving line of color. The amber green water through which they had been plowing seemed to have struck a barrier which was pushing it back, a barrier of deep green in which no amber showed at all. When Jeff Kennett exclaimed at this, Captain Bill Ballinger said, 'This is where you meet the sea, lad. Tide's on the flood and running strong. That's the sea water reaching in on us. Straight ahead is San Francisco.'

★   ★   ★

Jeff looked and saw the hills of the fabled city lifting. The mist of smoke dimmed its outlines and bits of fleecy fog scudded across the hill tops. Gulls, soaring on effortless wings, drifted and whirled above the *Flame*, uttering an occasional discordant cry. Then, as they drew closer, a forest of masts. Lining the docks, scattered up and down the waters of the bay, which seemed to run off into nothingness to the south, were hundreds and hundreds of ships. They were larger and loftier than any Jeff had ever imagined and made the squat, sturdy little *Flame of Sunset* seem puny by contrast.

Captain Bill swung the *Flame* south along the bay and soon they were in the midst of great numbers of small boats, bustling about between the shore and various ships anchored in deep water. All seemed confusion to Jeff and he thought half a dozen times they were going to run down one of these small craft, but by dint of short, angry blasts of the whistle, and copious and leather-lunged profanity on Captain Bill's part, they managed to get through without mishap. Presently they entered less congested waters and sidled up to an anchorage, some hundred yards out from the shore. The rusty old anchor on the *Flame*'s bow went down with a splash and presently she was swinging to it, quiet and resting.

Captain Bill turned to Jeff and said, 'Now to get ashore and sound out the beef market. Come on, we'll have a skiff put over and take a look at the town.'

As Jeff was about to follow Captain Bill into the skiff, Soapy came over, stripping off his gun belts. 'Put 'em on, Jeff,' he said. 'I won't need 'em here—but up town you might. I'm remembering that there Noah Carlin hombre is still on the loose and there is no tellin'. Put 'em on, so you'll have two of 'em and slung where you can get 'em easy. I'll take care of that pretty-pretty cutter you downed Taggart with.'

So the exchange was made and Jeff, when he stepped ashore, had the familiar feel of two good guns slung against his thighs. Then, as Captain Bill Ballinger led the way along to the main Embarcadero, they ran into such activity as Jeff Kennett had never seen before. A sort of surcharged energy was in the air. Piles of merchandise, fresh from the far ports of the world, bulged the doors of scanty warehouse space and spilled over in piles outside. Owners of this merchandise, despairing of a place of safety for it, and wary of thieves or the possibility of spoilage from weather conditions and only too anxious to convert some of it into ready cash, had auctioneers up, haranguing the crowds. Speculators, brokers and gamblers in these commodities shouted their bids, argued vociferously among themselves. Ponderous freight wagons lurched and creaked through streets which were a quaking morass of mud and sand and the drivers of these added their exhorting shouts at their laboring teams to the general uproar. Seafaring men in strange clothes moved about with their rolling gait and their voices sounded strange and foreign in Jeff Kennett's ears.

Captain Bill grinned. 'Well, what do you

think of it, lad?' he asked.

'Something about it that gets you,' said Jeff, his eyes shining. 'I've seen boom towns before, cattle shipping points out in Kansas, but they looked like what they were—boom towns that would disappear once the boom was over. Their noise was mostly that of wild living and general cussedness. This is different. This town will last. These people are really doing things, getting ready for the years ahead. They are people getting somewhere, people answering the call of a new, fresh empire. Man! I like this!'

They dodged the worst of the mud and started up Market Street. Here, too, seafaring men of all nationalities jostled and dodged laboring freight outfits coming and going. Stores of all kinds lined the street, and saloons were there in plenty. But here also moved men in cutaway coats and top hats. Here were sleek carriages, bearing fine ladies dressed in silks and satins. Here was the wildest hodge podge of humanity the world had ever seen. Yet, strangely enough it did not seem incongruous. For here was a brand new crossroads of the world. Here was San Francisco, final goal of a nation's bold trek of dreams to the west, into the sunset.

Captain Bill took Jeff by the elbow and steered him through swinging doors into the most ornate saloon Jeff had ever seen. The gleaming mahogany bar looked endless, with a massive mirror running the full length of the wall beyond. Pyramids of gleaming glassware on the bar shelves glittered in the subdued glow of hanging lamps. The bartenders wore spotless white jackets and aprons. Men were at the bar, men were at tables, lounging, drinking, talking. There was no loud talk, no boisterousness. Like the lights, the whole place seemed pleasantly subdued.

A man in business clothes, ruddy cheeked, with steady, alert eyes, came up from the back of the vast room and advanced with extended hand. 'Hello, Bill,' he said. 'Been waiting for you. Sort of figured you might be in today. Hope you got some cattle for me. I'm jumping that ante five dollars a head. I told you I would if the market held up.'

Bill shook hands and said, 'Meet Jeff Kennett, Charley. Jeff, this is Charley Rowe, the man I sold the cattle to, last two trips down. Charley, you're shaking hands with the owner of the herd, the man who brought that herd clear in from Texas—the hard way.'

Rowe's grip was firm 'A pleasure, Kennett, believe me,' he said with honest enthusiasm. 'Making that drive I consider one of the most remarkable achievements in this very remarkable country. I am happy to know you. I hope you considered the price on the first two loads of cattle as satisfactory?'

'More than I expected,' admitted Jeff honestly.

'You can't have all the two thousand head, Charley,' put in Captain Bill. 'Jeff is holding out five hundred to start a ranch with, up river.'

Rowe shrugged. 'That's all right. Good judgment on his part. Big future ahead in this country. But I'm still wondering, did you bring me a load of cattle?'

Captain Bill chuckled. 'We didn't come down just for the boat ride. How soon can you get your drovers ready to take over? I'm anchored at the same place. And the tide will be right in another hour.'

'My men will be there,' promised Rowe. 'I'll buy you gentlemen a drink and then we'll get about our business.'

Within half an hour Jeff and Captain Bill were back aboard the *Flame* and Bill went around giving orders. Presently several swarthy vaqueros came riding up to the shore and waited there, slouching indolently in their saddles. Then came a buckboard and in it was Charley Rowe. He cupped his hands and shouted, 'We're ready if you are, Bill. Turn 'em loose!'

Soapy came up beside Jeff. 'This will make your eyes pop, cowboy. Them cow critters done a heap of swimming at different times coming up the trail, but this is the first time they ever took off in salt water. Works like a charm. That Captain Bill—he's a corker. His idee. Claims he saw it done one time off a Spanish ship down the coast, only there the cattle had to swim a dang sight further than they do here. Slickest way to get shut of a jag of cattle I ever saw.'

A section of the heavy rail on the inshore beam of the *Flame* was lifted away. Then the deck hands, with prod poles and shouts, began forcing the cattle toward this gap. Those nearest it bawled in fright and alarm, but the pressure of the cattle behind shoved them off. They hit with a splash, went under, came up snorting and blowing, and, seeing sound earth close at hand, made for it, swimming sturdily. Long before the last of the cattle were off the *Flame*, the first were plodding up on the shore, dripping and gleaming in the afternoon sunshine. The vaqueros took them in charge, held them while the same procedure took place off the barge. It was over and done with in an amazingly short space of time, and then the deck hands got busy with hose and bucket, sluicing off and cleaning the cargo deck.

Captain Bill went over in the skiff and brought Rowe aboard. Rowe carried a small, heavy valise. Down in the cabin Bill said, 'Our count was three hundred and seven. What did you make it, Charley?'

'I got it three hundred and eight, one of

my men got it three hundred and six and another got the same as you. So I'll take your count and call it square. Satisfactory?'

'Plenty,' said Jeff. 'That was smooth work, Mr. Rowe.'

Rowe chuckled. 'Between Bill and me, we figure things out. Now for payment.'

It was in gold. It was counted and sacked and stowed away. Charley Rowe shook hands again, said, 'I'll be looking for more in a week or ten days from now,' and hurried away, a deck hand taking him to shore in the skiff.

Captain Bill rubbed his hands together and turned to Jeff. 'We can up anchor and pull out, if you say so, lad.'

Jeff shook his head. 'Tomorrow will be time enough. I've got to find some people in this town of San Francisco, and I don't know where to start to look for them.'

Bill's eyes twinkled. 'If those people happen to be named Sharpe, you might have a look at the Overland Hotel. Somewhere I heard they'd be staying there for a time.'

CHAPTER FOURTEEN

Two hours later Jeff Kennett stood in a hotel which was the most sumptuous he had ever seen. He walked across a foyer where the carpet under his feet was deep and soft. He climbed stairs covered with the same material and walked along a carpeted hall. As he knocked at the main door of a suite of rooms, he thought again how little he had dreamed, far back there in Texas, at the starting point of that long and toilsome and dangerous cattle-drive across half a continent, of what he would find at the end of that drive, here in this new and vigorous and vitalizing land of California.

The door opened, and it was Amanda Sharpe who stood there, her face furrowed with strain and stained with tears. She gave a strained little gasp, reached out and caught Jeff by the arm.

'Oh, thank heaven!' she cried, her voice catching in her throat. 'It's you, Jeff Kennett. Now at last perhaps we can do something—now perhaps we can find her.'

Jeff's face went bleak. 'Debbie! Something has happened to Debbie! What is it? Where is she?'

Amanda Sharpe pulled him into the room, shut the door. She dropped onto a chair, pressing her hands against her temples. 'I have to get it all straight,' she murmured. 'I've been half crazy with worry—and now I have to get hold of myself, so I can tell you exactly what has happened, so there will be no more time lost. Nate is no good in this sort of thing. He's out somewhere, running around like a madman, I suppose. But you—you will be able to do something. You'll be able to find her.'

Jeff's hand closed on the gray-haired woman's arm, hard and tense. He shook her slightly 'Tell me—tell me!'

'She—she went out for a drive, this morning. We could see no harm—no danger in that. The coachman was reliable—he's been with us for years, came out with my brother from the East. She was to be back for lunch, but she did not come. By mid-afternoon we began to worry. Her father went out to search, got men to help him. They—they found the coach down on the beach below the waterfront. The coachman was there, beaten to insensibility. Debbie—Debbie was gone. And—and we've had no word since. Oh, Jeff—Jeff—! This ghastly country—this terrible, ruffian filled—'

Jeff shook her again. 'The coachman—did he recover consciousness? Did he speak?'

The bent gray head nodded. 'There was little he could tell. He said that Debbie asked him to drive down this lonely stretch of beach, said she wanted to look at the bay. I think—I know that she was looking for—the *Flame of Sunset*, and you. Well, the coachman said that a surrey, with half a dozen men in it, came down the beach also and the feeling came to him that perhaps he and Debbie had been followed down from town. So he swung our carriage around and started back. This surrey blocked his way, the men leaped out and attacked him. He fought as best he could, but they beat him into unconsciousness. That was all he knew.'

'He did not recognize any of the men?'

Amanda Sharpe shook her head. 'No, he did not recognize any of them.'

It seemed to Jeff that he was freezing from the feet up. He was searching for thoughts and words when hurried steps came along the hall. The door was flung violently open, and Colonel Sharpe came dashing in.

Nate Sharpe was haggard and drawn. For all his weakness, his past venality, there was no doubt that he was suffering bitterly. His sister came to her feet. 'Nate—you've some word—?'

'Yes!' he almost shouted. 'Yes, I've word. The scoundrel! The ruthless, unprincipled scoundrel! He couldn't rob me when we dissolved our partnership, though he tried by bluster and threat. And now, through my girl—my daughter—he is prepared to blackmail me!'

'Nate!' quavered Amanda Sharpe. 'Are you talking about—Noah Carlin?'

'I'm talking about Noah Carlin! He has Debbie—somewhere. Yes, Noah Carlin has my girl. Here—here, read this. Just now, as I was coming back to the hotel some fellow slunk up beside me, pushed this into my hand and fled into the darkness before I could stop him.'

Jeff took the paper which Sharpe, in his agitation and anger, had crumpled in his clenched fist. Jeff spread it out and read:

Sharpe:
  Nobody ever ran out on a deal with me and got away with it. I want the Beaver, *the* Storm King *and the* Sierra Madre. *You want your daughter. When you deliver to me full title of ownership of the above three boats, you get your daughter back. I'll give you until Thursday to think it over. By that time I'll have found means to contact you for your decision on the matter. In case you think I am bluffing, I might remind you that a certain barkentine will be sailing shortly for the Spice Islands. The captain of that ship would like nothing better than to entertain a beautiful passenger. Quite a character, that fellow—quite a character.*

The missive was not signed, but no signature was needed. Jeff looked at Sharpe and said, 'What is this deal he is talking about? Give me the particulars.'

Colonel Sharpe had quieted somewhat. 'All Carlin ever brought into our partnership in the first place was the *Gold Camp*. It was my money which furnished the *Beaver*, the *Storm King* and the *Sierra Madre*. All are new boats, larger and faster than the *Gold Camp*. Carlin demanded title to all three as the price of releasing me from the partnership. It was sheer, high handed brigandage, of course, and of course I refused, flatly. Now he has taken this means—'

Nate Sharpe dropped into a chair, head bowed, shoulders slumped. Jeff knew a pang of pity for him. 'Things could be a lot worse,' he said. 'At least we know something of where Debbie is, that she is alive and no doubt well. And we have until Thursday. Today is Monday. A lot can be done between now and then.'

Amanda Sharpe was watching Jeff through misted eyes. 'Carlin,' she murmured. 'The man is evil—evil. What can you do, Jeff?'

Jeff spoke with an assurance he did not entirely feel. 'Plenty. First, I can take the whole story to Captain Bill Ballinger. He's a cagey old fox, Bill is. He'll have some ideas. Between now and Thursday we can run down a lot of trails. And of course, if nothing else pans out, then there is only one thing to do—let Carlin have the three boats.'

'We'd do that, of course—of course,' agreed Amanda.

Jeff said to Nate Sharpe, 'I'm keeping this note to show to Bill Ballinger. Now get a grip on yourselves. I'll be seeing you before Thursday.'

Amanda Sharpe followed him to the door,

pulled his head down and kissed him on the cheek. 'I bless the day you started from Texas, Jefferson Kennett,' she murmured.

* * *

Jeff found Captain Bill at the Eldorado, the saloon where they had met Rowe. He explained matters hurriedly and let him read the note. A cold and furious light burned in Captain Bill's blue eyes. 'The dirty, foul scum!' he rumbled. 'He found he wasn't man enough to take your herd away from you, so he strikes out in another direction for easy money. If he has harmed a hair on the pretty head of that fine girl, I'll get him if I have to follow him to the farthest edge of hell!'

'There'll be a pair of us, Bill,' said Jeff grimly, 'and I'll get there first. But now to find him. Got any ideas?'

Captain Bill stared into nothingness. 'A boat man always thinks in terms of boats,' he murmured. 'If he has something he wishes to hide, he instinctively turns to his boat. I would myself. So I'd say the first thing to do would be try and locate the *Gold Camp*. It must be around the bay somewhere, for this note shows that Carlin is here, somewhere around San Francisco. Ay! We'll look for the *Gold Camp*. Come along!'

They hurried out down Market Street to

the Embarcadero, where Captain Bill began dropping into one waterfront saloon after another. Here and there he spied men he knew and to whom he spoke for a moment. Jeff followed along quietly, having an inkling of what Captain Bill was about. Presently, watching, Jeff saw a stir of excitement and triumph shine in Captain Bill's face as he talked to a lank and bearded man who had boatman written all over him. Captain Bill's eyes were bright and hard as he came over to Jeff.

'Skinny Hall of the *Wanderer*,' said Bill. 'He says the *Gold Camp* passed him day before yesterday evening, while he was bringing the *Wanderer* in to berth. He said the *Gold Camp* was heading down somewhere into the south bay. Good enough! Now, back to the *Flame*, lad.'

Captain Bill's powerful oar strokes sent the skiff skimming across the dark waters to the *Flame*, still swinging quietly at her anchorage. But the boat came to life in a hurry as Captain Bill's big voice began giving orders. The *Flame*'s anchor hawser was attached to the barge and the towing lines loosed. 'We won't need the anchor where we are going,' said Captain Bill, 'and it will hold our barge for us until we are ready to come back for it.'

At quarter speed the *Flame* sidled out into wider bay waters. Then Captain Bill sent for

Andy McLain, his engineer. In short, terse sentences, he told Andy what was in the wind. 'You'll see that the word gets to all our boys, Andy,' he concluded. 'So they'll know what we're fighting for. Should we find the *Gold Camp*, we'll be outnumbered, but the boys won't mind a few odds, knowing the rotten swab Carlin has become. See that they understand, every man of them.'

Andy hurried away, muttering to himself, and Jeff watched Captain Bill swing the bow of the *Flame* until it pointed north. 'I thought,' said Jeff, 'that the *Gold Camp* was seen heading south down the bay.'

Bill nodded. 'Ay. It was. But I doubt Carlin will keep her there. Now that his note has been delivered to Nate Sharpe he'll know that Sharpe will have men looking for the *Gold Camp*. So it would seem to me that Carlin would slip north in the dark, up toward the delta country somewhere, so that a first search of the bay would not show the *Gold Camp* anywhere. That would strengthen his threat and make Sharpe more willing to come to terms. We could do little in the dark, searching the south bay, anyhow—for it is a big stretch of water, a big stretch. If we find nothing where we are going tonight, tomorrow in the daylight we'll have a look at the south bay.'

'If Carlin is heading north, maybe he has already done so and is out ahead of us.'

Captain Bill, tooling his boat carefully across the dark waters, squinted thoughtfully. 'Perhaps. Yet I do not think so. He would have to be sure that his note had been delivered to Nate Sharpe. Then, to slide through unnoticed, he'd be picking the late hours. No, I've a feeling we are ahead of him. At best it's but a gamble we are working on, a chance we must take.'

Slowly the *Flame* threaded her way through the congested shipping area and then began a faster beat of her paddle wheels as the upper bay opened ahead. Captain Bill stuck his head out of the pilot house and squinted at the heavens, where a scudding film of mist was blotting out the stars. 'Fog up there,' he muttered. 'I doubt it will come down before morning.'

Andy McLain, his engines throbbing steadily, came back to the pilot house to report that the word had been given to the crew. 'A mad bunch of men they are,' said Andy happily. 'In a frame of mind to whip three times their number.'

'Good!' said Captain Bill. 'You'll have boarding lines made ready, Andy. The *Gold Camp* is much faster than we are. It will be tricky business coming alongside of her. We'll have but the one chance and we must not miss. Have men ready to make those boarding lines fast, the moment we hit.'

Andy hurried off again and Captain Bill

went back to his pipe and his glowering thoughts. Jeff sought out Soapy and Sling and told them the story. He said, 'I never knew a better cause for gun work, boys. So we'll do our part that way. This is for keeps. I'll be looking for Noah Carlin, myself.'

They reached the place where the upper bay narrowed between dark headlands. There Captain Bill signaled for a speed which did little more than hold the *Flame* against the ebbing tide. Every now and then he would stop the engines entirely and let the *Flame* drift with the tide for a time, a still, dark bulk. And at those moments he would step out of the pilot house, stare off to the south, eyes and ears straining. Then back to the pilot house, the slow beat of the paddle wheels again until the *Flame* had gained back what the tide had taken from her. Then once more silence and drifting, watching and listening.

The strain of it pulled the nerves of Jeff Kennett tighter and tighter, and his thoughts grew so bleak he had to shake himself violently to gain some surcease. He remembered Debbie Sharpe as he had seen her sitting in the carriage in Sacramento and he had crossed to talk to her. He remembered how dainty and fine she had seemed, how her face had colored so richly warm, how her shy glance had dropped. And he thought of her that night, under the oaks, so slim and vibrant, and the breathless sweetness of her mouth as he had kissed her.

Jeff shook himself again and stared out across black waters to the south, his eyes coldly bitter. The hatred of Noah Carlin which swelled in him was the deadliest thing he had ever known.

The slow, cold hours crept by. Stop and drift, look and listen, then beat slowly back against the tide to regain the distance lost. Captain Bill was holding the *Flame* in the very middle of the channel, dogged in his gamble.

Once more the *Flame*'s engines stilled, once more she drifted, once more Captain Bill came out beside Jeff to look and listen. And it was when Bill was once more about to step into the pilot house and signal slow ahead, that Jeff exclaimed—'Wait, Bill! What's that?'

Bill spun around, head cocked, hand cupped about his ear. The sound was faint but distinct. The pound of a paddle wheel, the sibilant cough of exhaust. 'Boat coming!' snapped Captain Bill. 'Stern wheeler and without lights. This could be it! Pass the word, Jeff. Get the boys on their toes.'

Captain Bill stood in the door of the pilot house, watching, waiting, letting the *Flame* drift. If this approaching craft was the *Gold Camp*, then success or failure of the whole venture lay squarely on his judgment, on his craftiness at the wheel. Failure could bring disaster in more ways than one. If he let the *Flame* drift squarely into the path of the other boat, then the *Flame* could very well be crushed and sunk. Or if he missed his lone chance at laying the *Flame* alongside, the faster boat could pull away easily.

Bill Ballinger's blunt jaw stood out, his eyes went cool and settled. He waited, listening, watching.

The beat of the approaching paddle wheel grew louder. And then Bill's straining eyes picked up the dim, dark bulk of the boat and he marked the lines of superstructure and cabins. He let out his breath in a gusty sigh. The *Gold Camp*! And on a course to send her by but a few yards off the port beam.

Captain Bill leaped for the wheel and signal cord. Bells jangled in the *Flame*'s engine room. Full speed ahead! And down there a waiting and watching Andy McLain gave the *Flame* everything she had. Her paddle wheels thrashed and foamed, halting her drift. She shuddered and creaked at every seam. Then she began sliding ahead, faster and faster, and Captain Bill spun his wheel hard to port.

Now for the first time the *Gold Camp* seemed aware of what was in her path. Her whistle growled angrily and she started to swing away. But Captain Bill had maneuvered just the edge he needed. The

Flame drove angling at the larger craft like an angry bulldog, and came alongside with a solid emphasis that sent timbers to grinding and squealing. And Captain Bill held her there, boring in—boring in.

A scurry of dark figures catapulted over the *Flame*'s cargo deck rail and onto the cargo deck of the *Gold Camp*. Heavy hawsers they dragged with them, to loop about the mooring bitts of the *Gold Camp*. When a wild yell signified that this had been safely done, Captain Bill stopped the *Flame's* engines, tore out of the pilot house and drove savagely toward the battle that had already begun.

Jeff Kennett was in the first group of men to hit the *Gold Camp*'s cargo deck. Soapy and Sling were close at his heels and Jeff caught Sling by the arm. 'Stay right here,' he yelled. 'And kill any man who tries to cut or throw off those ropes. Kill any man who comes near them! All right, Soapy—this is Texas coming!'

Soapy answered with a long, shrill Texas yell, and rushed forward at Jeff's shoulder.

A dark tide of men came charging at them. With cold, savage purpose, Jeff and Soapy stopped that charge and broke it to shreds with snarling, deadly guns. This blast of flame and death was something the *Gold Camp* crowd had not expected. They scattered and ran, cursing their terror. But they left crumpled figures behind them.

Jeff sped for the upper deck and was near the top of the ladder when a dark figure loomed above him. Jeff swung low and back and the flailing club that had been swung at him barely missed before crashing down on the metal hand rail. Jeff drove a slug into the center of that figure and it fell away, gasping. Then Jeff surged on up into the clear, with Soapy at his heels.

Down on the cargo deck the *Gold Camp* crew had formed for another rush and this time Captain Bill Ballinger was there to lead his men. He led them mightily, roaring like a berserk lion, swinging fists like post mauls, finally grabbing a club away from a cursing figure and using it like a flail.

A dark figure came slinking in at one side, to make a sudden rush for the mooring bitts, an ax swung high. Sling shot the man dead in his tracks before the ax could fall. It was a lesson quickly learned, no more of the *Gold Camp* ruffians trying for the lines.

Up above, Jeff and Soapy closed in on the pilot house of the *Gold Camp*. From it gun flame lanced and Jeff felt the wind of the slug past his face. He drove a shot back and a second one. But the gun from the pilot house snarled again and again and behind Jeff, Soapy came down all asprawl, cursing furiously.

'Go get 'em—go get 'em, Jeff,' yelled

Soapy. 'Just my leg. Go get 'em!'

Jeff laced the looming bulk of the pilot house with both guns, driving in low and crouched. Glass tinkeled and shattered and two dark figures burst out of the place.

One of the figures was Noah Carlin and Jeff did not need clear vision and daylight to know it. The recognition was instinctive. He cut down at Carlin and the gun snapped empty in his hand. He tried the other and knew he had missed, tried again and it also snapped empty.

Carlin and his companion came at Jeff. A knife gleamed palely, swung high. But back there on the deck Soapy's gun snarled and the knife wielder gasped a strange, foreign sounding curse, stumbled and slid forward on his face. Then Carlin swung a furious blow at Jeff.

Jeff hunched a shoulder and took it there. It made his whole arm numb and drove him to one side, hard against the pilot house. But he came back, lashing out with the empty gun he held in his right fist. The first blow caught Carlin on the forearm, snapping it like a pipe stem. Jeff went after him, swinging again and again. Carlin gave ground, for this was an indomitable, coldly purposeful killing machine coming at him.

Back Jeff drove him, back and ever back across the upper deck, until Carlin came up against the rail. Stark fear ran through Noah

Carlin now. Behind him were cold, black waters and a racing tide. The sweat of terror broke from every pore.

Carlin tried to dodge along the rail but Jeff headed him off, gun held high, waiting his chance to lash out with a finishing blow. In sheer desperation, Carlin tried to upset Jeff with a sudden rush. He came in, sound arm flailing. Jeff took the blow so that he might land one himself. Carlin's fist and Jeff's gun barrel landed simultaneously.

Jeff staggered and reeled, half stunned. But he knew that gun barrel had landed solidly. Dimly he saw Carlin whirl away, driven by the blow. He saw Carlin hit the rail, jackknife over it, then slide from view. Below there was a heavy splash, then no sound at all.

Jeff went back to where Soapy lay gritting his teeth and knotting a faded neckerchief about his wounded leg. Jeff dropped on one knee beside him, still panting from his efforts.

'Where's Carlin?' rasped Soapy. 'Don't waste no time foolin' with me, Jeff. Go get Carlin!'

'Carlin's—done for,' Jeff gulped. 'I gun-whipped him and he went over the rail. Carlin's through.'

Men came surging up from the cargo deck, with Bill Ballinger in the lead. He was yelling—'Jeff—Jeff!'

'Over here!' answered Jeff.

They came crowding around, gleeful with victory. 'They got a bellyful, quick—down below,' panted one *Flame of Sunset* valiant. 'But Carlin is the man we want. Where is he?'

Jeff told them and for a moment they went still. Then Bill Ballinger summed it up grimly. 'He asked for it. Now to find that girl.'

'If she is aboard, I think I know where to find her,' said Jeff. 'The same cabin Carlin had me locked in. But first, Soapy downed a hombre over yonder. He was with Carlin in the pilot house. He came out swinging a knife and when Soapy dropped him he was mumbling in some foreign way.'

One of the men brought a light. The man with the knife was dead enough—a short, thick, bearded man with gold rings in his ears. Captain Bill said harshly, 'Carlin meant what he said in that note, Jeff. Here, for a dollar, is the man who would have sailed that barkentine for the Spice Islands. If I'd had any regret at all for Carlin, which I didn't, I'd have none now. He's where he belongs. Send this fellow after him.'

Men lugged the limp figure away. There came another dull splash.

Jeff led the way to the cabin where he had been held. The door was locked. Jeff knocked and called, 'Debbie—Debbie! This is Jeff—Jeff Kennett!'

They heard her little wail of joy and the beating of her small fists on the door. 'Jeff! Oh, Jeff darling! I'm locked in. I can't open this door—'

'Stand aside, lass,' Captain Bill called. 'We'll take care of that. Stand aside. We're coming in.'

Captain Bill braced himself, put his massive shoulder to the door. It creaked and strained, then gave with a crash, the lock shattered.

There was a scurry and then a slim figure had hold of Jeff, clinging to him, laughing and crying, her soft hands going over his face in fluttering little pats of endearment.

'Hold me, Jeff—hold me. Don't ever let go of me again—!'

CHAPTER FIFTEEN

With the barge at tow again and the white caps dancing and slapping under her forefoot, the *Flame of Sunset* plowed a sturdy way north across the bay. It was a crisp, bright afternoon with the feel of autumn deepening in the air. The *Flame* was a happy boat this trip, for several reasons. One was that Noah Carlin was now a threat forever done with. Noah Carlin had come to a deserved end under the waters of the bay and the *Gold Camp* was in the hands of the Port Authority, awaiting future disposal.

In the crew's quarters of the *Flame*, Soapy was resting at ease, his wounded leg having been taken care of by the best doctor in San Francisco, and Soapy had that worthy's word for it that all the leg needed now was rest and a chance to heal. With Sling to keep an eye on him and keep him company, Soapy was content. And up in the pilot house, Captain Bill Ballinger was sucking on his pipe, a foot on the wheel, his blue eyes resting fondly on the two people standing forward on the upper deck—Mr. and Mrs. Jefferson Kennett.

Debbie was hugging the arm of her tawny haired young husband, re-explaining a few things.

'I was a silly idiot, of course, darling. Aunt Amanda told me I was, for sending you away. But I was deeply ashamed, because of Dad. I knew he had his weaknesses, but I had never dreamed he would let a man like Noah Carlin make such a fool of him, make him almost—a scoundrel. When I found out what he and Carlin were scheming against you, I thought I would die. I could not see how you could help but despise me, for I despised myself. And so, it was shame which made me send you away.'

Jeff squeezed the small hand which lay in

the curve of his arm. 'But what was your heart saying, Debbie?'

She looked up at him shyly. 'You heard my heart when I answered from that cabin, Jeff. And the vows I made just these few short hours ago must convince you, my husband.' Then she laughed, gaily mischievous, like a little girl. 'Poor Aunt Amanda—poor Dad. The swiftness of it all just about floored them, didn't it? I don't believe Dad fully realizes yet that he has lost a daughter but gained a son. And Aunt Amanda, she would have liked a very impressive ceremony, under considerably more dignified surroundings.'

'Like they would do it in Boston?' grinned Jeff.

'Exactly. But you must admit, when she fully understood our mood and determination, she was a brick.'

'Aunt Amanda,' vowed Jeff, 'is the pure quill. She'll do to ride the river with, any old time. I'm plenty fond of Aunt Amanda.'

Debbie's hand tightened ever so slightly on Jeff's arm. 'And—and Dad—?'

Jeff stared soberly, straight ahead. 'I'm remembering your father as he came into the hotel, after searching everywhere for you, and after receiving that damnable note from Noah Carlin. He had only one thought, one concern. You. Nothing else mattered. He and I were on common ground, then, good solid ground. We'll stay there. Your father and I will get along.'

Captain Bill leaned out of the pilot house and his big voice came rumbling. 'I know the world is one big rose garden for you two, with little pink angels fluttering around. But don't forget your old friends entirely.'

Debbie laughed and blew him a kiss off her finger tips, then said to Jeff, 'Go up and talk with that old bear, darling. I'm going down and sit with Soapy for a while. He is one of my boys now.'

Captain Bill, puffing furiously, watched her dart away. 'All the brightness and joy of the world is in that little lady, Jeff,' he growled. 'If I ever hear of you speaking even one unkind word to her, I'll wring your confounded neck.'

Jeff smiled. 'If I ever do, you can, Bill. But I been wondering, old timer—what are you going to do when the last of the herd have been hauled to San Francisco?'

'Hah!' grunted Bill, 'I've already taken care of that. Charley Rowe, who's been buying your cattle, has quite a business head on him. He bumped into an auction down along the Embarcadero the other day. Feller had a whole setup of saw mill machinery. Seems it came around the Horn by ship on consignment to some jigger who got into a cutting scrape in a dive on Pacific Street and came off second best. With nobody to claim the machinery, the ship's skipper was trying to get at least the freight costs out of it. Anyhow, Charley Rowe bought it up, cheap. He's aiming to set up a mill somewhere up river, maybe on the Feather or the American River, where he can float logs down from the timber stands higher up in the hills. Sawed lumber, Charley says, is even more scarce and hard to get in San Francisco than beef. There is some coming in from the redwood country north along the coast, but not near enough to meet the demand. I'm to haul the machinery up river for him and then haul lumber back. So it looks like the old *Flame* has got herself a steady job ahead. And when that new ranch of yours begins producing enough beef to make it worthwhile, well, you just holler and old Bill and the *Flame* will be dropping by for a load.'

'You'll be dropping by long before then,' said Jeff. 'I'm going to need quite a jag of lumber, myself, what with a ranch headquarters to build. And if it is going to take just business to get you to call in on Debbie and me, then we might as well move on deck and have it out, right here and now.'

Through the darkness and the light, the *Flame* foamed sturdily on and berthed for a time at Sacramento. A visit was made to Lizzie Jackson. When she heard the great news, Lizzie smiled wisely, kissed both Debbie and Jeff and insisted on a bountiful supper in celebration. It had been in Jeff's mind that Debbie stay with Lizzie Jackson until he had a chance to set up some kind of comfortable accommodations for this slim, gay young wife, at the site of the new ranch headquarters to be. But Debbie would not listen to it.

'I'll have you understand, Jefferson Kennett,' she declared, 'that I did not marry you to be packed away in cotton like some fragile piece of bric-a-brac. I seem to remember coming clear across the plains from Ft. Leavenworth, riding a saddle every step of the way, sleeping on the ground with only a tent to cover me. And none the worse for the experience. Where you go—I go. And that's that!'

Captain Bill chuckled hugely. 'That's a good lass. Spur him and make him understand early, who is boss.'

So, when the *Flame of Sunset* nosed out into the channel and continued on up river, Debbie was there in the pilot house, eager and enchanted when Captain Bill let her handle the wheel where the waters were broad and deep. Often, too, she would stand far up on the bow of the *Flame*, where the breeze would whip tendrils of her silken hair about her face, and exclaim like a delighted child as flights of wild fowl thundered up from some back water and set their curving wings against the sky. She seemed to wait with tiptoe eagerness for each turn of the river to disclose some other new fascinating vista.

Debbie was on the bow when, as the *Flame* foamed around yet another turn, a group of riders appeared ahead, swimming their mounts across the river, faces taut and grim, weapons held high out of the wet.

'Stony—Stony!' yelled Jeff Kennett.

The riders plunged up the west bank, dripping. When Captain Bill stopped his engines and let the *Flame* nose gently in, Stony Peters was already calling the news to Jeff.

'That Don Carlos hombre, Jeff. He's trying to raid the ranch herd. Buck Yarnell sent word for us to come arunnin'. Things are pretty stiff going, I reckon!'

There were three horses on board—Jeff's, Soapy's and Sling's. While the *Flame* was being solidly berthed and the gangplank run out, Jeff and Sling were feverishly saddling. Debbie, who had scrambled into riding clothes, came running. She was a trifle pale, but definitely determined. 'Jeff,' she cried. 'I'm going with you. I'm taking Soapy's horse.'

'No!' growled Jeff. 'This is work for men. No, Debbie, you stay here.'

Her eyes met his, very grave and steady. 'Where you go, my husband—I go. It must always be that way. Sling, saddle Soapy's horse for me.'

She had her way and when, along with Stony and the rest, they went racing away from the river toward the broad plains beyond, Debbie was riding at Jeff's elbow, with Sling, faithful and watchful, spurring along at her other hand.

* * *

Far out ahead they could see that the conflict was already taking place. Tiny, mounted figures were dashing back and forth and faint puffs of smoke told of gun work going on, though the combination of distance and the drumming of racing hoofs muffled any sound of report. Between Jeff's group and where the fighting was going on, there were cattle, cattle frightened and wary and scattered, and Jeff saw what doughty old Buck Yarnell and his tiny group of valiants were doing. They were trying to hold a line between the raiders and the cattle, trying to keep the cattle back close to the river, where the raiders could not get behind the animals and stampede them out into the vastness of the wide plains.

So far, it seemed, Buck and his boys had been successful, but even as he watched, Jeff saw a group of speeding riders swing south and disappear into the green barrier of growth along the watercourse on that side, while still another group was swinging around to the north and east. Buck Yarnell, it seemed, had stopped them in the center, but he did not have the men to defend those dangerous flanks.

Jeff threw up his arm, reined in. His orders were quick and curt. 'Stony, take three men and swing north and break up that gang coming in from that side. Sling and I and Hod and Rio will take on those who just ducked into the willow along this creek to the south. Go get 'em.'

The group split, raced away. Jeff doubted that the raiders had yet noticed his group, for the timbered line of the river bank was just behind them, and riders would, until farther away from the river, be more or less indistinguishable against that background. Jeff did not cross the watercourse to the south, but instead kept his little group close up against the willows and alders and pin oaks which lined it, while driving forward at a furious pace. He reasoned that the raiders who had disappeared into the creek cover, had crossed to the far side and would be coming down along it over there, confident that they would meet up with no opposition when they recrossed to the north bank to get at the cattle. Knowing the value of surprise in a thing of this sort, Jeff figured to utilize this advantage to the fullest.

He glanced at the slim figure speeding at

his side, and knew a keen pride. Debbie's eyes were shining, her cheeks full of color. Here was no slightest fear, only a vivid loving of excitement and movement. He knew a gnawing worry for her safety, yet was aware that he could not have held her back. She had said that she would ride at his side, regardless, and it was plain that nothing could change her in that.

She felt his glance and met it and gave him a flashing smile. Jeff leaned over and called against the rush of air, 'There is danger up ahead. Do you realize that?'

'Yes,' she called back. 'I realize it. If you can ride into it, I can—and will.'

Presently Jeff reined in and spoke to one of the men, who cut swiftly into the willows, down and across the creek and up the far bank. Shortly he was back.

'Coming with a curl in their tails,' he reported laconically. 'About four hundred yards up stream. Be even with us in a jiffy, now.'

'We'll wait right here,' decided Jeff. 'If they cross below us, we'll drive them into the river.'

Over where Stony had gone, guns had begun to crack, the reports thin and far away. Jeff stood in his stirrups for a better look and what he saw made him swell with pride. Stony and his little band were charging straight in, riding low in their saddles, shooting as they went. No jockeying for position, no fancy maneuvering for Stony and those good boys. They were going in as purposefully as a straight punch to the jaw, and Jeff saw Don Carlos' vaqueros begin to scatter and swing away.

Sling, also watching, drawled with a faint, grim smile, 'Chunk of Texas hell in the saddle out there, Jeff. No yellin', and fancy ridin' and shootin' in the air. Just cold turkey—plenty cold. Somebody is due to get a lesson they won't soon forget.'

That shooting which Stony and his boys had begun carried to other ears, also, for up the stream a little way and on the far side, a voice rose in brief alarm and with a volley of orders. Willow clumps crashed under the pound of hoofs. Then came the splash of water in crossing, then more crashing as riders came plunging up the near bank.

Out of the willows, not fifty yards ahead, broke a group of vaqueros. In the lead was a thick, squat figure which Jeff quickly recognized as Don Carlos in person, looking and pointing out across the range to where Stony and his boys were driving a bunch of vaqueros in wild flight.

A high, shrill, Texas yell came from the throat of Jeff Kennett. Don Carlos jerked around in his saddle and saw thundering straight at him still another group of unsuspected Texans.

The surprise was complete. A gun snarled, smoking in Sling's ready hand and, right beside Don Carlos, the catlike figure of his nephew, Don Luis, bent at the waist, swayed, and toppled out of the saddle.

The vaqueros scattered like quail, swinging back into the willows, spurring their mounts madly. Don Carlos tried to do likewise, but his horse, stung by another bullet, bolted straight out across the plain. Jeff Kennett, yelling an order, went after it in a surge of wild speed. While he rode, Jeff reached, not for a gun, but for the lariat strapped at his saddle horn. He got it free, ran out a loop, reared high and forward leaning in his saddle, lifting the last ounce of speed from his scudding mount, while he measured distance with a calculating eye.

Don Carlos' horse was very fast and Jeff saw in an instant that in any extended run it would draw away from his own pony. He'd get a chance for just one throw and that would be all. He swung the loop twice then sent it writhing snakily out. For a moment it seemed the length of the rope would not be enough. But when the loop spread and settled, it just did reach, with Jeff helping by the fullest stretch of his outthrust arm. Jeff sat back and jerked. The loop snapped tight about Don Carlos' body and he came backward out of his saddle, squealing like a caught rabbit. He hit hard, bounced and rolled over and over. Jeff, leaping from his saddle, took one long stride. He was standing over Don Carlos when the latter collected wits and breath enough to struggle to his knees. 'I warned you, Don Carlos,' Jeff said coldly. 'I warned you. Now we'll see!'

Hoofs pounded up beside Jeff. It was Debbie, and now at last was she slightly pale and shaken, for she had seen Don Luis die swiftly under the lash of Sling's gun, and in the fixed expression on her husband's face she read doom for this squat and terrified man on the ground.

Jeff put a foot against Don Carlos' chest, pushed him flat, then went over him swiftly, plucking a knife and a revolver from him and tossing them aside. Then he loosened the loop of his lariat, lifted it higher and twitched it snug about the Don's fat neck.

'All right,' Jeff rapped. 'On your feet. No tricks, or I'll drag you from here to the river at the end of this rope. Where I came from we have but one medicine for cow thieves, or would-be cow thieves. That medicine is a rope and a tree.' He went back into his saddle and twitched at the rope. 'Get up!' he snapped. 'On your feet. You asked for this.'

Don Carlos staggered erect. Jeff looked around. Shooting had stopped. Sling and Hod and Rio were already coming back out of the creek cover and when they rode over to Jeff, Sling reported in disgust, 'Only thing they got worthwhile is high class horse flesh. They went away from us like we were tied to the ground. But not a lick of fight in 'em, with the odds anywhere near even. What you aim to do with that one, Jeff—stretch him?'

Jeff nodded and Debbie caught her breath in a little gasp.

Stony Peters meanwhile had given up pursuit of the vaqueros he had gone after, for they, like the others, were making the best of their superior horse flesh. Now Stony was circling toward the battle line which Buck Yarnell had been holding. Presently they were all coming back and as they drew nearer, Jeff counted, rigid and cold until the tally was complete. The only bandage in evidence was around Buck Yarnell's head. But the wound could not have been much, for old Buck's eyes were clear and fierce and unquenched in spirit and energy.

At sight of Don Carlos on the end of Jeff's rope, Buck started to swear in grim satisfaction, but broke off in some confusion as he spied Debbie. Jeff chuckled.

'You better mind your manners, you godless old cactus burr, else your new boss will ride you bug-hunting. Which is as good a time as any, I reckon, to make all you boys acquainted with Mrs. Jeff Kennett. Debbie, this is the crowd of wild junipers you'll have to ride herd on. And I warn you, they're a flock of horse thieves.'

'They are not,' retorted Debbie indignantly. 'They're—they're grand—just grand.'

'Hah!' rumbled Buck Yarnell. 'Hah! Fine young whelp you are, keeping things from me and the rest of the boys.' He looked at Debbie, doffed his battered old hat with a quaint courtesy and said, 'Ma'am, your slightest wish is our command.'

Debbie rode right over to Buck, her lips quivering just a trifle, her eyes misted. 'Your head. You must let me tend that wound.'

Buck's eyes grew very soft. Right then and there did Debbie crawl into his gruff old heart forever. 'It's nothing to bother your pretty head over, lass. Just a scratch. That gang couldn't shoot worth shucks. We did a little better.'

'How many did you get, Buck?' asked Jeff.

'Four. We got them on the first rush. After that they kept pretty well out of range. But I knew they intended pulling a surround, so I sent one of the boys after Stony and the others. Didn't expect you to arrive when you did. I see you got the main squeeze.' He nodded toward Don Carlos.

'Yeah,' said Jeff. 'And Sling got Don Luis—the gent with the thirsty knife.'

Buck stared at Don Carlos. 'You already got the rope on him,' he growled. 'There's an oak tree yonder that will hold him.'

Don Carlos went into a spasm of almost

tearful pleading, wringing his hands. Buck said contemptuously, 'Shut up, you lily livered whelp. We don't know what you're saying in that lingo.'

Then everyone was startled, for Debbie said quietly, 'He says that if you will spare him, he will never trouble you again. He swears it. He says that he has been very, very foolish and that he is sorry and will pay in full for any damage done.'

She changed to fluent Spanish and spoke at length to Don Carlos, while Jeff and the rest listened, amazed at her command of the language. Don Carlos kept bobbing his bullet head, saying something over and over again. He was sweating and trembling.

Debbie turned to Jeff. 'You will not, as Sling put it, stretch him, darling. You will let him go. I have told him, however, that if ever he or any of his men do bother us again, I will not intercede for him a second time.'

Jeff was silent. Debbie rode over to him, dropped a hand on his arm. 'This, our new ranch, is a beautiful land, Jeff. We must not lay a shadow across it, by—by hanging that terrified creature. Please, Jeff—'

It was Buck Yarnell who reined over, loosened and lifted the noose. Buck growled, 'You lied to Jeff and me, Don Carlos—and still live. But now you have given your word to a good and generous lady. You better keep that word. For if it ever turns out that you have lied to her, then you'll certainly swing. And that's a solemn promise. Git!'

If Don Carlos did not understand the words, he certainly understood the tone. He scuttled away, panting and mumbling, with a backward look. Buck turned to Jeff. 'All right with you, younker?'

'All right, Buck,' Jeff nodded. 'The lady wins—and I'm glad.'

Debbie looked at Jeff, at Buck, at all of the riders, and said with simple directness, 'I love you—all of you.'

★   ★   ★

They gathered on the little knoll above the river, among the patient oaks. Captain Bill and his crew came up from the *Flame*. They built a fire and prepared a meal. While this was going on Debbie heated water and made old Buck Yarnell sit quietly while she washed and bound up his wounded head. Soapy, carried up from the boat, lounged at ease on a pile of blankets and traded good natured raillery with the rest of the outfit. Plans for the layout of the new headquarters were discussed. Buck Yarnell pulled Captain Bill aside and said, 'When you're rammin' around down in that there San Francisco place, you keep an eye open for anything in the way of house furnishin's that will make things nice for our little lady boss. She's entitled to everything that's best, and by gollies she's going to have it. Me and the boys aim to foot the bill.'

Over where Soapy lay, Stony Peters was saying, 'One thing them jiggers has is high class horse flesh. I saw one up on a palomino that was a wonder. I aim to get one just like it for the missus, if I have to steal it.'

Debbie had good ears. She picked up these low toned comments, and her soft lower lip trembled and her eyes misted. She looped an arm in her husband's and said, 'They're sweet, Jeff.' Then she added, with that faint, almost impish smile. 'You better be good to me, darling, or they will, as Soapy would say, make you hard to catch.'

Jeff grinned fondly. He took one of her hands, looked at it. 'Soft little hand,' he murmured. 'Yet you hold all of us in the hollow of it, sweetheart.'

Later the two of them moved up to the very crest of the knoll, stood looking out to the west, where the range lay tawny gold under the last rays of the declining sun. Debbie stood in the circle of Jeff's arm, her head burrowed against his shoulder. And so they watched the sun go down beyond the distant blue mountains, against a backdrop of rose and scarlet glory.

'Flame of sunset,' murmured Debbie. 'Way back across the desert I used to watch that sunset and wonder what it held for me. Now I know. The pure gold of happiness.'

L. P. Holmes was the author of a number of outstanding Western novels. Born in a snowed-in log cabin in the heart of the Rockies near Breckenridge Colorado in 1895, Holmes moved with his family when very young to northern California and it was here that his father and older brothers built the ranch house where Holmes grew up and where, in later life, he would live again. He published his first story—'The Passing of the Ghost'—in ACTION STORIES (9/25). He was paid ½¢ a word and received a check for $40. 'Yeah—forty bucks,' he said later. 'Don't laugh. In those far-off days ... a pair of young parents with a three-year-old son could buy a lot of groceries on forty bucks.' He went on to contribute nearly 600 stories of varying lengths to the magazine market as well as to write over fifty Western novels under his own name and Matt Stuart. For the many years of his life, Holmes would write in the mornings and spend his afternoons calling on a group of friends in town, among them the blind Western author Charles H. Snow whom Lew Holmes always called 'Judge' Snow (because he was Napa's Justice of the Peace 1920–1924) and who frequently makes an appearance in later novels as a local justice in Holmes's imaginary Western communities. Holmes's Golden Age as an author was from 1948 through 1960. During these years he produced such notable novels as DESERT RAILS, BLACK SAGE, SUMMER RANGE, DEAD MAN'S SADDLE, and SOMEWHERE THEY DIE for which he received the Golden Spur Award from the Western Writers of America. In these novels one finds the themes so basic to his Western fiction: the loyalty which unites one man to another, the pride one must take in his work and a job well done, the innate generosity of most of the people who live in Holmes's ambient Western communities, and the vital relationship between a man and a woman in making a better life.

The employees of G.K. HALL hope you have enjoyed this Large Print book. All our Large Print titles are designed for easy reading, and all our books are made to last. Other G.K. Hall Large Print books are available at your library, through selected bookstores, or directly from us. For more information about current and upcoming titles, please call or mail your name and address to:

G.K. HALL
PO Box 159
Thorndike, Maine 04986
800/223-6121
207/948-2962

LP Holmes, L
Hol Flame o

FEB 1 01
AUG 21 01
FEB 11 03

2811
3621
4249

HICKMAN COUNTY PUBLIC LIBRARY
EAST BRANCH
LYLES, TENNESSEE